<u>Confluence</u>

Ron Mueller

<u>Books by Ron Mueller</u>

The Savitar Series-Science Fiction
- Journey's End
- Savitar
- Confluence

Bram Nielson Series-Science Fiction
- The Fold
- The Message
- Fold Wormhole
- Negative Fold
- Ripples in Time

The Alex Evercrest Series-Detective
- The River Front
- The Girl on the Grill
- Missing
- Maggot
- Racist
- Votive Candles
- Windy City
- Country Road
- Pool of Blood
- Sins of the Daughter

The Taelo Series-Prehistory America
- Taelo: The Early Years
- Taelo: The Golden Feather
- Taelo: Journey of Discovery
- Taelo: Dangerous Passage
- Taelo: Condor Clan Slingers
- Taelo: Circumvention
- Taelo: The Journey of Sages

A Taelo Story
- The Name of the Child
- White Swan and Quiet Pheasant
- Broken Spear
- Floating Cloud
- Quiet Rabbit
- Busy Bee
- Little Otter& Talking Wren
- Burley Bear & Meadow Flower

A Feather-in-the-Wind Story
- The Eastern Elk Clan

The Door Series-Science Fiction
- The Door
- Delivery
- Journey Beyond

The Problem Solver Series-Secret Agent
- The Beginning
- Drug Lords
- Broder Crosser

Current Past and Future-Science Fiction
Event Survivors-Science Fiction
The Door-Science Fiction
Viajante 7-Science Fiction
Imagination - Courtney Huynh & Chloe Parker

Confluence

By: *Ron Mueller*

Around the World Publishing LLC
4914 Cooper Road Suite 144
Cincinnati, Ohio 45242-9998

This story is a work of fiction. Names, characters, places, and incidents either are products of the author's imagination or are used fictitiously. Any resemblance to actual events or locales or persons, living or dead, is entirely coincidental.

Confluence by Ron Mueller, Copyright © 2019.
© 2021, renewal April © 2023

All rights reserved, including the right of reproduction, in whole or in part in any form.

ISBN 13: 978-1-68223-307-8
ISBN 10: 1-68223-307-3

Cover Picture by: Hannu Vitanen - Dreamstime.com
Cover Design By: Ron Mueller

Ron Mueller

Confluence

Table of Content

Ron Mueller

Confluence

Chapter 1: Astounding Discovery

The Savitar was now functioning as an Earth escort and a science project platform. Zack had been elected the first President of the Savitar. He had positioned the Savitar as a neutral entity to be considered the Switzerland of Space. The relationship between Earth and the Savitar was evolving and various countries desired to have formal ambassadors and staff on the Savitar, but Zack was inclined to keep the political structure lean and at a minimum.

Zack and his leadership team decided that an Earth Ambassador representing the entire Earth would be appropriate but the staffing for that ambassador had to come from the people who were already on the Savitar.

This approach caused a mixed response but eventually the UN agreed to establish a post with one person who would be elected by the representatives in the UN.

Zack and the leadership team were pleased with the final arrangement.

Living space on the Savitar was limited and managing the Savitar to remain a viable entity was a task that kept all inhabitants totally engaged. Without exception person on the Savitar recognized that their life was better than the ones they would have had on Earth.

Life was as good.

Zack was proud of the active engagement his teams had with various teams on Earth. These teams were critical in bringing the critical skills and capabilities up to the Savitar.

Craig's team asked to give the Savitar's leadership team an update on a new discovery. They showed them a series of pictures indicating that a previous intelligence had traveled the solar system. They displayed a series of pictures taken on the Savitar's journey that had been studied in detail.

He pointed out the evidence showing that a previous civilization had traveled through the solar system. He and his team had discovered this almost by accident but after their initial find on Mars they had found evidenced in pictures that the Savitar had taken as it had come out to capture the blackhole.

His team had kept it under wraps until they were absolutely confident of their findings.

He then said put in a request.

"Gentlemen, we are sharing what my team and I feel very certain that we have discovered. We have found signs of a previous intelligence. There are indications on Mars, on the moon of Jupiter and most clearly on a moon of Saturn.

The request that I am making is to utilize the equipment of the Savitar to scrutinize the moon of Saturn and determine if a full project expedition should be sent to investigate it more closely," Craig said as he put the pictures with the evidence in front of Zack and Enrico.

"Such a discovery would be astounding. It is hard from these pictures to conclude this is the case. What am I missing," Zack asked as he took in Craig's request?

"Here, see the rows along the wall of this deep canyon. This is a picture taken of a deep mantle canyon on Mars. This seems to suggest there are multiple floors cut into the mantle.

Now look at the picture of Europa, a moon of Jupiter. See this huge post. It appears to be some sort of giant anchor with a ring at the top. It is almost totally buried in the ice, but we were able to enhance the picture to see it more clearly. It appears to be fabricated and put there for some purpose we have not yet determined.

Finally, look at the ruins of some giant structure on Titan the largest moon circling Saturn. We did not see it until we were able to screen out the thick cloud cover.

This picture seals my belief of some intelligence traveling our solar system in the distant past." Craig said as he explained the pictures to the group.

"Let's agree to the exploration of Titan as our first scientific investigation. I am not sure I am bought into Craig's interpretation of the pictures but investigating and learning about our solar system is what we are about." Zack commented to the leadership team.

Enrico nodded in agreement and made the official proposal to travel in toward the orbit of Saturn and send a scout out to Titan for a closer look.

The leadership team agreed and the first scientific journey for the Savitar was put into swing.

Enrico suggested that the Savitar would move part of the way toward Saturn, but it had to stay far enough away to prevent any undesired effects the presence of the Savitar might have. Having a captive black hole worked well to provide the Savitar with an almost perfect one G gravity but it still exerted its presence on the paths of the various objects in the solar system.

Captain Rajkumar of the Rama eagerly volunteered his ship as the perfect match for the task at hand.

The leadership team agreed and suggested that the team that would do the exploration decide what they needed and start to prepare the Rama for its first excursion.

The journey to Saturn was much slower than the journey out to the black hole. They were now moving carefully and staying away from the orbits of the planets. And moving the Savitar meant determining where they might be going next after their move toward Saturn.

Confluence

Currently the Savitar's travels were synchronized to the match the speed that the Solar system was moving. It chose to slow down just a bit and move toward the Saturn just a bit. A bit was the best they knew how to communicate what a slight deviation was to be. They were still in the learning process of pushing the black hole in the direction they desired.

The Rama was made ready for the exploration of Titan.

The Indian crew was excited to be the ship to be named to be engaged in the first exploratory mission. Their community had several celebratory gatherings to celebrate with the crew.

The leadership team had agreed that Craig would lead this first expedition.

The Rama was capable of landing on the surface and taking back off from Titan. This would allow for firsthand exploration.

As the Savitar got closer to Saturn, they verified earlier analysis of the makeup of the atmosphere and the seas of Titan to be a methane-ethane mixture.

It was in essence a sea of gasoline. This was an obstacle to the plans of landing on to the surface.

The Rama would not be able to land after all. Their engines would potentially ignite the atmosphere and the seas.

New plans went into full discussion,

The powerful telescopes scoured the surface of Titan. The ability to filter out much of the cloud cover allowed Craig and his team to examine the surface of Titan. They spent almost a month meticulously examining the surface.

The day the scene of the surface revealed a ring in the surface ice of the moon a cheer went up from Craig and his entire team.

They took a series of pictures and then compared it to the picture of the other ring that they had taken on Europa. The ring was a duplicate.

Craig brought it to the leadership morning meeting and made the point that the second ring confirmed the existence of a previous intelligence.

Zack complemented Craig on his team's thorough and correct analysis.

"You would have to have a mighty big dog to hook his chain to that ground ring," Janet joked as she stared at the ring.

Her comment caused Zack to jump up in excitement.

He pointed at Janet and said that she was a genius. She had just described a ring to hook a space elevator to. It is the anchor point of a cable. We of all people should recognize it. The Savitar is held together by cables. We rode up and down on the welding elevators for several years. There were huge rings at the ends of those cables.

How could I have missed it when Craig first showed me the pictures?"

It made sense. The previous visitors would not be able to land their spacecraft, but they would be able to hook up and set up a space elevator and then visit the surface.

They could not chance using the existing ring since they did not know its true condition.

They would need their own anchor.

Analysis of the atmosphere and the gravitational attraction showed that the Savitar would be able to land a glider near the existing ring.

They would design a similar anchor to which the Rama would connect. The expedition would then go down to the surface in an elevator. The solution was simple but executing it would be a new experience.

They would need to construct the elevator container and the motor system to run it up and down. They decided that the downward power would be the weight the elevator and the upward pull would come from a cable hooked to a motor on the Rama.

The crew of the Rama promised that they would be able to hold the elevator line stable. They simulated keeping the Rama in place as the various forces they were able to measure affected them.

They practiced as they traveled out to Titan. As they approached they declared that they were ready.

The news about the discovery when it hit the Earth was electrifying. The data sent back by the Savitar was now poured over as the various experts looked for additional evidence.

Every University and research department wanted access to the data and began to scrutinize it and scour it for indication of a previous civilization.

The satellites, placed around Jupiter and Saturn as the Savitar went out to the black hole, were now programmed to examine the larger moons. Each of the major moons would have every square foot examined in multiple frequencies.

The Mars satellite began to examine the cliffs more closely on the deep canyons. They began to provide additional evidence of this previous intelligence.

The exploration of the exterior structure on Titan was carefully examined. The structure appeared to have been an enclosure designed to shield those inside from the atmospheric pressure. Titan's atmospheric pressure was sixty times greater than Earth's. The expedition going to the surface of Titan would require suits capable of withstanding this pressure and providing a suitable internal environment for the individual. An exoskeleton design was selected. The person essentially became encompassed like a turtle.

Getting to the surface would not be as difficult as initially anticipated. Gravity was weak enough that a human could almost fly by beating their arms.

However, the concept of an elevator was more practical. The concept of a space elevator was not new. It had never been tried because of the extreme length of cable required for an Earth space elevator. The one for Titan would still be very long but the Savitar had already broken the mold on the size limits. They also had the two-hundred-forty mile long pull cables used to pull the Savitar full size cables into position.

These were the right length and tensile strength required for an elevator to the surface of Titan.

The fact that the Savitar had several spare cables that could be used greatly shortened the preparation time for the team to get to the surface.

This was an expedition that energized Craig. But he wanted to be the technical leader. He realized that someone else should be the mission leader.

One of the young marine lieutenants reporting to Captain Moffett was selected to be the mission leader. He would be responsible for the logistics and safety of the team when on the ground. He would take his direction from Craig about the actual investigation.

Craig would guide the scientific aspects of the mission. The team consisted of a four-person camera crew, three scientific analysts, four support personnel, Craig, and the mission leader.

The final design of getting the cable to the surface of Titan was labeled the Harpoon. From synchronous orbit the Rama shot the harpoon to the surface of Titan.

The force and the heated tip drove the harpoon forcefully into the ice. Spikes shot out in radial direction from the shaft to lock the harpoon in the ice. Two of the team members glided down on the thin pull cable. They carried six additional anchors down with them.

Once on the surface they permanently positioned the initial anchor by retracting the radial spikes and sinking the main shaft to its maximum depth. They then reset the radial spikes. The six additional anchors were positioned in a circle around the harpoon anchor and sunk at an angle with their tops coming together near the Harpoon anchor. The pull cable was threaded through the eyes of the anchors and the end was sent back up to the Rama.

The team back on the Rama fed out the line until they had the end back. They then began to feed down the elevator cable to be attached to the anchor point.

Craig waited impatiently for this activity to be completed. He was anxious to get to the surface. The atmospheric cover made it impossible to get a good view of what was on the surface.

Finally, the elevator was ready.

The team would descend together except for two of the support members who would bring down the additional equipment and supplies.

The structure was within five minutes walking distance from the ancient anchor. Walking was not really the right word. It was more of a skating motion. If too much energy was put into a step the person would launch themselves off the surface. It was much more of a motion like cross country skiing.

Craig had often engaged in cross country skiing and spent some time training his team.

Soon everyone was moving smoothly toward the ancient structure and the anchor.

They approached the ruins of the immense structure carefully so that they would not disturb any of the surrounding debris.

They stood outside of the structure and carefully took pictures. The part of the team back on the Rama and viewing the pictures commented that there seemed to have been rooms inside the structure.

There was a feeling of extreme age. The pyramids felt young as compared to what Craig felt as he walked around what he surmised was the interior.

He was carefully making his way around what seemed to be the perimeter of the structure when what he saw made him stop in his tracks. Directly ahead of him was a twenty-foot diameter circular area on the floor that seemed to be a cover.

He approached it and carefully examined it. He could see no way to open it or go down around it.

They would need to bore down and see if they could go around it to see what was below.

Next Craig led the team to the anchor just outside of the structure. It was indeed exactly that. The material was not metal. It appeared to be a highly stable and structurally sound type of ceramic. It was pitted, and it seemed and felt to be extremely old. On one side of the ancient anchor was what appeared to be hieroglyphic symbols.

Just below the writing was a small, sealed chest of the same material as the anchor. Craig did not know the contents of the chest, but he imagined the contents were intended to communicate with the finder of the chest. The chest had a black spot in one corner. The spot appeared to be a seal to a hole.

He immediately called for a container that could be vacuum sealed so that he could send the chest up to the Rama. He had the person that would handle the chest sterilize his gloves before touching the chest and putting it into the container. Once it was ready it was sent up to the Rama. He would take it back to the Savitar and use all the technology available to examine the interior. In the near future, he could envision himself carefully opening the chest in the confines of a sterile clean room.

He and the team returned to the structure and the circular cover to what he imagined would be a tunnel descending vertically down into Triton. He had the team examine the area around the cover.

There had to be a way around it or perhaps at one time the cover was lifted from above. There did not appear to be any exterior connections for lifting. Craig thought about it and decided it was probably designed with a failsafe mentality. This would mean the cover would be lifted from below and upon failure of the lifting system would seal itself from its own weight.

He decided trying to get past the cover should wait until the equipment to get past the cover without contaminating the interior could be brought down on a future trip. He had his team take measurements and pictures but instructed them not to move or disturb anything.

He decided that he needed to get some archeologists to take charge of this project.

After three days on Triton the team had a complete map of the structure and precise measurements. It was time to leave. The anchor set up by the Rama was left in place. Future expeditions would be able to send down their connection cable and utilize the anchor.

Zack was waiting on the Savitar when Craig returned. He watched as Craig escorted the container with the ceramic chest to the clean room in the science lab.

"We will need to design and review the process to be followed in opening the chest. Here is what I believe we will find.

The black ceramic spot has material inside to allow us to establish the age of the chest.

The chest itself will have ceramic discs or other materials with the information about the race leaving the message. It may also have some sort of high-density information media. That is what I would leave behind if I was permanently leaving the solar system." Craig shared with the Savitar leadership team.

"President Lansing has sent up a message saying he would like to send up a team to study the Triton site. Your theory of life on Mars seems to have been verified by additional passes of the satellites over the area where you found the cliff dwellings. There is now a massive effort on Earth to send a team to Mars.

The satellite around Jupiter is now examining the three largest moons to see if there is any indication of visitors on them." Zack shared with Craig.

"It seems we will be busy for the foreseeable future studying the artifacts of the race that made it out here ahead of us."

Once again Zack's world had changed.

It was hard to believe that in his lifetime he had captured a blackhole and put it to use. Now the Savitar had discovered an ancient set of visitors or perhaps the first intelligent beings in their Solar system. Had this intelligence developed on Mars as Craig was now proposing?

He knew that somehow the blackhole that now was part of the Savitar had been involved in what had happened to these ancient beings.

He held Janet's hand as they walked around the garden and knew that he would be going out in search of these previous space travelers to learn more about the history of his home world and its solar system.

Neither of them had envisioned this as the next adventure but both of them were committed to finding out if such a solar system history existed.

Chapter 2: Visit to Mars

Zack and Janet established a research team to dig into the history of the Solar system. This after all had been the thesis for Zack's PhD thesis. His original focus had been on catastrophic occurrences that had affected the Earth. All the research and study that had been done to document the catastrophic events in Earth's past took on a new perspective.

The fact that the black hole might have influenced the events on Earth as well as Mars and the missing fifth planet now had to be considered. Zack knew that his thesis might be partly incorrect because he had not even considered the possibility of a blackhole affecting the events on Earth.

Zack had not looked at the solar system as a whole and he had not considered the presence of a blackhole. That presence could in fact have been the cause of many of the catastrophes that plagued the Earth.

Zack got support from President Lancing and reconstituted the Pathfinder analysis program that had been discontinued when the Savitar plans dominated and consumed the globe and its resources. Now it made sense to look again at the data they had previously gathered.

Zack suggested that the black hole that he had captured might be the reason that Mars was in the terrible shape it was in. Perhaps the black hole and the planet had in the distant past interacted. He asked the analysis team to determine the time that it took for the solar system to go one time around the edge of the Milky. He wondered whether every two hundred million years the black hole interacted with the solar system. It perhaps was the culprit for many of the solar systems ailments.

The answer to the time around the milky way was roughly two hundred and twenty million years.

Alex, Craig, Janet, Susan, and Mitch looked at each other and then they once again looked at the time frame they were discussing.

The possibility that the solar system had spawned two intelligent species was mind blowing.

It was hard to believe, and it was humbling to know that an intelligence had potentially developed space travel more than two hundred million years before the human got down from the trees and took their first steps.

This meant that Mars would have developed intelligence during the first age of the dinosaurs!

Mitch commented that he wondered what would have happened if the black hole had not existed and had not interacted with the Martians, would the Martians be in control of the Earth and its people?

Zack was certain that the small blackhole that was now the center of the Savitar had been the reason for the dramatic damage that Mars exhibited. It was clear that Mars had suffered an earlier dramatic impact that had cracked its mantle. So Mars seemed to have experienced multiple catastrophes.

One of the team members postulated the theory that the destruction of the fifth forming planet was disrupted by the black hole and this had sent a piece out that was large enough that when it hit Mars it cracked the mantel. The impact also affected Mars core and its magnetic field.

Craig and most of the analysis team thought it was a miracle to have intelligent life arise in such an environment. They also thought that the beings would have had to have been a tough lot to escape and survive in space.

Craig asked Zack to organize and plan the effort of discovering what was sealed in the ceramic time capsule.

He said that if as he thought, it was more than two hundred and twenty million years old, then it should not be opened unless those opening it were sure that they would not destroy the information that was sure to be inside.

Janet immediately volunteered to be part of the effort. Mary and Jeff both volunteered as well. All three of them had been working with Dr. Garrity on the investigation of the ceramic box.

Janet said that there was some strong pull about the box that she was not sure she understood but she definitely wanted to be on the team to investigate it.

Zack in discussion with President Lansing established a team that had numerous Earth-bound scientists and the team aboard the Savitar working together. This was an arrangement that ensured keeping Earth engaged in a positive and constructive manner.

This team would have multiple goals.

One goal was to plan how to proceed in learning what was in the ceramic chest and what was below the gigantic circular seal down on Titan. These two elements on its own their own were monumental tasks.

The second goal was to set up an expedition to Mars and get boots on the ground and determine if there had indeed been a civilization there in the past. This activated the exploration support part of the effort to learn about the Martians.

The third goal was to plan for the exploration of each of the other moons that had evidence of previous Martian visits.

Each goal would have separate teams assigned and staffed.

Janet became the project leader for the Savitar contingent that would go to Titan and explore what was below the circular seal.

Craig would lead the direct examination of the ceramic chest with the goal of learning what was inside.

Zack was going to be involved in all the efforts, but he did not have full time to invest. He was the first President of the Savitar and was involved in the politics of getting the Savitar government fully functional and dealing with the interface to Earth.

Craig was the ambassador from Earth to the Savitar and Zack had to constantly remind him of that fact. He suggested that Mary Ringhold and Jeff Mallory should take on a greater role in the investigation of the Ceramic box.

Craig grudgingly acknowledged this fact and did as suggested.

Craig reviewed what needed to be done to get the box examined and eventually opened. He made the point that he did not know if the box would be opened in his lifetime.

He stressed the fact that the team had to take all precautions to ensure that they would not damage what was in the ceramic box.

He, Mary, and Jeff developed a draft investigation plan that entailed using all the available non-invasive technology that they could think of.

This plan was reviewed with their Earth counter parts and with the Savitar leadership.

The Rama was assigned once again to be the ship that would go to the Triton and tie to the anchor.

Zack had requested that the sea be tested to see if the Savitar could utilize it for fuel. If it were feasible, he wanted to create a fuel reservoir on the Savitar. This would ensure that they would have a supply for their engines. He asked Conrad Zepf to lead this effort.

The ceramic Bucky ball production system was producing two thousand Bucky balls a day. These were being used to create the floor for another of the many open pentagons that made up the Savitar's one G level.

Sampson had been one of the people that had saved Zack's life. He now got to do whatever he wanted.

Zack asked to Sampson take charge of utilizing each day's production of bucky balls and get another section of the Savitar covered.

Zack had rewarded the "Boss" and his team of workers by giving them the work they desired. This had been the group that had developed the self-propelled, computer driven welders that had saved the Savitar from destruction when they went around the moon on their departure from Earth.

The "Boss" was an excellent supervisor and the people working for him respected and had become his supporters. They excelled in the work they did for him.

The "Boss" was in charge of the construction of the facilities on the ceramic pentagon. He had all the required materials. The majority of what he was responsible for building was to be made of the ceramic sheet, bars, and planking. He, however, had the full range of plumbing, electrical and air conditioning that took a mix of materials.

The ceramic pentagon as it had come to be called was being built in record time.

Zack had expected such an outcome. He had the two best people leading the efforts.

He had plans to isolate the housing and equipment for opening the ceramic box in the middle of the newly covered ceramic hexagon.

He thought it appropriate that the Ancient ceramic treasure box left by the mystery space travelers would be isolated in the middle of a totally ceramic based part of the Savitar.

Craig and Janet became an inseparable team as together they planned the investigation of the ceramic container and the facility on Triton.

They engaged a full range of experts to figure out how to get around the seal to what they thought would be a shaft going vertically into the ground. They worked together to identify all the equipment needed to get around the seal.

They worked with another set of experts to determine how to handle the ceramic box. This team faced a monumentally challenging task. No one knew how they were to handle the chest if the chest was as old as it was thought to be.

Though Zack had all the burners on high it still would take a significant time to get the Triton team ready and supplied with the equipment needed. Some of the equipment was coming from Earth and that took more than six months just in transit time.

The team to examine the ceramic box faced the same issue. They had a CAT scanner, a PET scanner, and a wealth of other equipment also being sent out from Earth.

President Lancing had said that several specialists were also coming to the Savitar and were planning to stay for the duration that it took to examine the box and solve the mystery of who had transited the solar system in the long past.

Zack had a laugh when the several was close to one hundred scientists. The Savitar could handle the increase in population but he realized that it would continue to get requests for additional people to come to the Savitar.

Zack studied the photos taken of the deep chasm on Mars. As he studied additional photos, he became convinced that the beings that had traveled the solar system originated on Mars. He was sure they had faced the black hole now at the center of the Savitar.

They had apparently left the solar system after their inability to establish themselves on the various moons.

He asked Janet if she were interested in seeing firsthand the origin of the beings that had most likely drilled a shaft down on Triton. The two of them decided to take a ride on the Sprite when it returned to Earth to ferry the people from Earth to Mars.

This would give him an opportunity to visit his family and once again put his feet down on Earth.

Janet insisted they also go to Hawaii where she wanted to walk the beach with him.

Zack kissed her and said he would love to and asked if she would marry him once again when they walked the beach in Maui.

Craig heard about the plans and decided to join as well. Emily was ecstatic. She knew that she of all people was truly bound to the planet of her birth. She had become quiet famous as a Chef on the Savitar and was immediately sought after by a wide following back on Earth when word got out about her visit.

The four of them estimated that their time away would give the project to examine the contents of the box and to visit the Triton facility the time it would need to get ready.

Space aboard the Sprite was reserved for them and the plans for their arrival on Earth were underway.

President Lancing was on his last year of his second term. He planned to honor Zack with a parade and a formal dinner event. This was something that he had not anticipated when Zack and the Savitar had departed some six years prior.

Now that his term would soon be over he was eager to meet face to face with both Zack and Craig and discuss the possibility of immigrating to the Savitar. He, his wife and the rest of the family had discussed this and come to the conclusion that for him it would be a great new venture.

Zack and Craig each spent time studying every picture from Mars. A robot had been landed and was making its way along the chasm. The photos from it immediately convinced both of them that they were looking at a vertical city built into the mantle.

They were now impatient to get there.

They convinced the President to allow the Sprite to make a brief stop on Mars before coming to Earth.

The President's approval meant they would be the first humans on Mars and the first to examine the ancient artifacts that were there.

Zack, Craig, and Janet were ecstatic. Emily told everyone that she was not sure she wanted to go down to the surface of Mars. She commented that she was sure they would be visiting a tomb where many people had died.

She had no idea how right that was, but she also had no idea what two hundred and twenty million years would do to any tomb.

The trip to Mars drove home the point that the current design of spaceships was of an inadequate and ancient design. The designers of the current generation of spaceships were planet and gravity oriented.

The designers of future space craft needed to be space oriented

The gravity orientation needed to be ship oriented.

He and Craig discussed this in great detail and decided they would sponsor a rotating structure design that would simulate gravity inside the spaceship.

The trick would be to get their design to feature ships with gravity like forces in a small structure and to do it in a practical, economical way.

They conferred with a design team back on the Savitar as they journeyed toward Mars.

On their arrival to Mars, Zack had the Sprite position itself over the area in the cracked mantle and slowly move along its length.

The Captain Moffet, Zack and Craig all let out a yell as their telescope showed a hole in the ground.

Image enhancement revealed another anchor deep within what seemed to be a missile launch tube. This once again was evidence of a Martian race of beings.

It was an intoxicating learning beverage. The talk constantly went to what these being might have been like. What was their body structure? How did they think? Did they walk erect similar to a human. Where they bigger than Earthlings.

The discussions and questions seemed endless.

Zack requested permission to go to the surface of Mars to verify the presence of an anchor and whether the Sprite could utilize it.

Captain Moffet chuckled as he declined Zack's request. He apologized but said he could not let the President of the Savitar go gliding down to the surface. It would be much too risky.

He instead named three of his people to go down and plant a new anchor for the Sprite to use. Once the anchor had been planted and the Sprite had a functioning space elevator down to the surface Zack and his contingent could descend.

He went on to state that Zack and each of the three would have two of the Sprite's crew members be their support personnel.

Janet knew Zack well enough to know he was super energized about getting to the surface to determine if their indeed had been intelligent life so long ago.

She was just as excited and could barely wait but she also sensed that their findings might haunt them. She anticipated the history of the place was a history that at its final moment had a multitude of deaths associated with it.

She made a joke about the fact that wisdom came with time but the amount of time that they were involved in was beyond comprehension and maybe they would find themselves to be senile before they unraveled their two hundred-million-year mystery.

Zack agreed and said that he was not going to wait until he was that old and planned to find the Aliens or their remnants in his lifetime.

Zack and Craig conferred with the rest of the team members to plan what they would do when they got to the surface.

They all agreed that they would descend into the tube where the ancient space anchor was located. They would then see if they could go beyond that point.

Janet stopped the discussion and made the point that airports and missile centers on the Earth were usually initially positioned outside of city centers where the population was the lowest. This would mean the anchor location they were contemplating exploring might be far removed from the high-density location. She suggested that they place the anchor as close to the edge of the canyon crack in the mantle as possible.

Zack and Craig agreed with her logic and thanked Janet for her suggestion. They once again examined their pictures and decided that the location of the anchor was a fair distance from the crack in the mantle.

They requested a change to where the Sprite's anchor would be located. It was agreed that the location would be several hundred yards from the edge of the crack in the mantle.

They asked Janet to pick the spot she had in mind. Janet carefully examined the rim of the mantle crack and zeroed in on a spot that seemed to have been created by something more than nature would have done.

Little did she know that she had selected the spot that had been the favorite location for the person that had led the Martian Survival after their confluence with the blackhole and would soon become Janet's obsession.

Chapter 3: The Discovery of Ulm

Three of the Sprite's personnel descended to the surface. There was not enough atmosphere to support a parachute descent. Instead, a small roto-blade vehicle that used a huge parachute with three-foot holds that each person stood on was used to slowly lower the three persons to the surface. The vehicle was navigated by an on-board computer. It gently brought them down to the ground. Once they were down they proceeded to go to where the anchor was to be located.

Janet commented that they looked much like a swan gliding in for a landing.

The cable to thread the anchor had come down with the three. It had been attached to the top of the parachute as a safety line in case there was any problem on the descend.

The anchor was shot down to the surface and the three manually finished securing the anchor and threading the pull line.

This anchor had been loaded with a rotating drill much like the drill on an oil rig and the time it took to drill the anchor down to the designated depth was a direct indication of how hard the surface happened to be.

Captain Moffit commented that the hard rock might make it a little longer to set the anchor, but he said it meant a better anchor point for the space elevator and that made him feel much better.

Once the anchor was set, the same roto-blade vehicle that brought them down was then sent back up with the thread line. This last maneuver almost failed as the Martian atmosphere thinned. However, a contingent plan was for the entire vehicle to use a small rocket to push it up to the Sprite.

The large space anchor cable was then slowly pulled down and secured.

Zack, Janet, and Craig in full space suits came down the space elevator cable on a small platform. They met the three crewmen already on the ground and proceeded toward the edge of the canyon. Three additional support personnel came down the elevator next.

Looking over the edge of the crack gave Zack acrophobia. He was overwhelmed at the depth of the fissure in the mantle. He took several steps back and got his balance back.

He and everyone take a step back from the edge. They all commented on the extreme depth of the chasm.

Janet walked over toward a glint that had caught her eye and stumbled. She had tripped on what seemed to be a metal object. She backed up and tried to see what she had stumbled on.

Closer examination and brushing the soil aside revealed that it was the edge of a ring that seemed to have a forty-foot diameter. Everyone worked together to expose the edge of what seemed to be a cover to a tube. They all agreed that it was similar to the cover on Triton.

This energized everyone. Craig said that for him it was solid proof that the Martians had been the ones to make the journey out to Triton.

Janet knelt and put her hand on the surface. She had tears of emotion in her eyes. Even the capture of the blackhole had not touched her as much as finding the remnants of another civilization was doing.

One of the crew men had wandered off and then called out that he had found the top of an open shaft.

Craig went over and suggested it was the top of an elevator shaft. It appeared the top area had been ripped off.

The team requested that the Sprite send down their elevator repair crew. This of course was a joke, but Captain Moffet understood the request and sent cabling and the material to make a platform that could be lowered down the shaft.

While the makeshift elevator was being assembled, Zack and the rest of the team brushed off the fine dust and sand that had accumulated on the forty-foot diameter cover.

It had what they took to be Ulm engraved on it and some additional lettering that they could not read.

They took digital pictures of the writing and the cover and sent these off to be studied.

Zack hoped that the linguists folks would figure out the Martian alphabet quickly.

The makeshift elevator was completed, and they all got on and rode the shaft to the very bottom. They counted almost two hundred "elevator" stops that could be investigated.

Zack and Craig postulated that they were passing the levels of floors. They both agreed that manufacturing and production would be at the lowest level. The precious space at the floor of the crack would be for raising food.

They all got off the elevator when it reached the bottom. There was a short hallway that led to the exterior.

Janet was in the lead. She realized she had assumed her protection position. She had been in that role for so many years that it had become second nature to her. She chuckled when she realized what she was doing. She turned to ask Zack where he wanted to go.

Zack was looking through his binoculars past where she was standing. He commented that they should walk toward what seemed to be a tunnel.

Craig came to a stop and turned to ask what Zack was looking at.

He turned back around to proceed forward but stumbled over something in the dust. He and one of the crewmen dusted off a plague with writing on it.

Janet realized they were standing at the opening of a long tunnel back into the mantle. She point in and asked what they were looking into.

Zack squatted down and peered in as far as he could see. He asked one of the crew men to shine a light into the tunnel. The dust layer seemed to thin down as it went farther into the tunnel but even at the opening there seemed to be bumps under the dust layer. The bumps were spaced close together and seemed to form a pattern similar to bumps that would be on a plush rug.

The opening to the tunnel had some sort of frame. The team proceeded along the right wall of the tunnel and made sure not to step on any mound they encountered.

Finally, Janet knelt down and with a light brush carefully brushed the dust aside. Everyone let out a quiet gasp as the remains of a body took shape.

Emily had been right in her anticipation of going down and finding out she was walking among the dead.

Janet gazed back toward the opening and knew they had found the resting place of thousands of the people that had lived on Mars.

A shiver went down her back and she felt the spirits even after so many millions of years.

Zack had the three crew men go farther into the tunnel and then take pictures back toward opening. He asked them to send them up to the Sprite for transmission to everyone involved.

He turned and led the way back to the opening. There he stopped and looked at the ceramic sign that was now leaning against the stone wall with its base resting on what he believed was a transport platform. He took a picture of what was written on it and sent it up to the Sprite.

He then had the plague prepared to be sent up to the Sprite.

He, Janet, and Craig discussed what they should do. Zack was now convinced that there had been an advanced civilization on Mars long before the human race had come into existence. And he felt certain that the three of them were standing in the place where it had all started.

He wondered aloud why they had not migrated to Earth.

Janet pointed out the significant difference in gravity and the barrier that would have for the Martian race.

She then brought up the point that they had been able to stay out in space without losing anyone because of the nano-bots that now resided within them and repaired the radiation damage. She wondered if the Martians had nano-bots.

She identified with the frustration the Martians must have had in seeing a thriving third planet that they could never set foot on.

Craig voiced a desire to see how far the tunnel that they had been focused on would go.

Zack decided he wanted to go up through the mantel structure and see what could be learned of the vertical housing design.

They decided to split into two groups and meet back at the shaft up to the surface in eight hours. That would put their time on Mars to twelve hours.

He asked the two crewmen that were taking the plaque up to the surface to return with three scooters for Craig's group.

He then said that he and Janet were going to figure out how to climb back up the levels to see what they could learn.

Once the scooters arrived Craig had about six hours of time before needing to be back. He led his team toward the tunnel. He wondered what he would find.

Zack and his team were on foot. He was not sure how his team would negotiate their way up through the various levels of the structure he was now referring to as Ulm.

He and Janet led the way through a small door opening into the interior. They each carried a powerful light. Janet was happy that there were no bumps on the floor of what appeared to be a long hallway.

Zack shined his light into one large area. He asked Janet what she saw.

Janet immediately thought of a lab but on closer observation she realized it was an indoor garden area. There were still pots on various shelf locations and there appeared to be long rows of what could have been shallow water ways.

She took pictures that she planned to send back to Lisa.

Zack agreed. He had spent many hours in Lisa's garden areas. This was almost a duplicate of what she had up on the Savitar.

He went farther down the hallway. He hoped to find stairs that would lead up.

The stairs he found had him put the size of the Martians at about a third taller than Earthlings. He had already reached that conclusion from the bodies he had seen in the dust, the height of the hallways added to his certainty and now the step height sealed it for him.

Janet agreed with his conclusion.

They agreed to go up for what they thought would be the halfway mark and that they would stop if they found something especially interesting.

Janet made the observation that some levels had bodies randomly spread out while others seemed to be clear.

Zack agreed with her observation. He postulated that some floors may have been designated as cemetery areas while some floors were used after the destruction by the blackhole. This implied that there had been some survivors on the surface of Mars. The space anchor they had seen from the Sprite was probably the location of the final departure of the survivors.

Their upward journey took them from what appeared to be work areas, into areas that were living spaces.

Then at level ninety they entered an area that both Janet and Zack agreed reminded them of a park. They decided to walk through the "park." As they did so they realized that the ceiling was at least four to six levels above them.

Zack laughed and said he was back in Harvard. Janet replied that he was wrong, and it was her university in Baltimore.

They walked into an area that clearly had been a library. They were both sure they were on the grounds of a large university. The layout, though carved out of rock, clearly spoke of an educational institute. The monumental volume of the area was overpowering.

Janet had tears in her eyes as she looked around at what she was sure was the heart of the people that had lived here so many millions of years before. It was having an impact that she had not anticipated. There was something that fused that distant past to her own experiences.

She could not separate what she was exploring with all her personal experiences when she had gone to her university. She was drawn in by the grandeur she imagined had existed in the area around them.

These beings had risen to a height of learning that was comparable or maybe higher than what had been achieved on Earth. They had lost it all when they encountered the blackhole.

She looked at Zack and knew that Earth had him to thank for averting a similar fate. Earth was also lucky to have been just slightly more advanced than she thought the Martians were when they encountered the black hole.

She planned to walk the beaches of Maui with her white knight and soak up the emotional wealth that she knew she would experience. Having made the descent to the surface of Mars and gotten a better understanding of the fate of the many beings that had lived on it, would make the Maui walk on the beach seem like a miracle.

She would once again look into the saltwater pools among the volcano lava. The teaming life of crabs, small fish and seaweed would all continue indefinitely because Zack had envisioned the Savitar and Earth had the time, the technology, and the resources to avert the fate of the Martians.

The Martian race did not have the technology or the resources, but she was sure it had its heroes or heroine that had led them through the solar system.

Going up the stairs had been a physical challenge. Going down became an emotionally challenging one. It seemed that tears kept continually running down her cheeks.

Zack commented that there was a century of study and learning for Earth scientists that was to be had in the small area they had explored in the last several hours. When these scientists came to Mars, he was sure that there was a wealth of knowledge that would reward the Earthlings.

Craig was amazed at how far the tunnel went. His team was traveling about fifteen miles per hour. They seemed to pass a tunnel that went back into the mantel about every ten minutes.

After three hours of travel, they came to another area that seemed to be a city. The tunnel continued on.

Craig carried on a running commentary about what he was seeing and his interpretation of it.

His two companions were mostly silent but would periodically point out some feature. One such feature had been what they called a train. They were sure it was a train engine laying on its side that stood out prominently at the entrance to one of the side tunnels.

Their comments and discussion had him looking at the floor over which they were moving. He soon spotted what he thought of as bolt holes to hold a rail. He wondered what could have cleared the tunnel so effectively.

He hated to turn around, but he ran out of time before he ran out of the tunnel. It was clear to him that the tunnel had been a transit route. It probably had a rail that ran its length. He thanked his two team members for seeing the train engine.

A train engine! The thought just kept recycling. This was the location of a thriving community. What had wiped it out of existence?

The three of them stopped at the entrance where the train "engine" was located. It was hard to verify what the lump might have been, but it was large enough to be a train engine.

Craig was about to return to the main tunnel when his light illuminated what he took to be a bank vault entrance. It was clearly a massive door.

He led the way to what he called the door. It was massive. He could barely squeeze his way past. His light only illuminated the area close to the door, but he was sure he was inside of a survival chamber. He wondered how many Martians had survived.

He wished he had more time to explore but he needed to honor the time commitment for his return. He knew that future explorers would examine and estimate how many survivors had been saved by the massive doors.

He gathered what appeared to be stones at the side of the tunnel and built a cairn to mark the entrance. He took a picture and commented that it marked the location of what he believed was a survival chamber.

He turned and went out and led the way back to the meeting place.

The discussion about what they each had seen exploded as the six made their way to the surface.

Zack, Janet, and Craig all agreed that the Martian civilization had achieved space travel at least two hundred million years before humans populated Earth.

Even now human space travel was at its infancy. Would they have been able to do what the Martians had achieved?

Craig threw out the question about where the Martians were now, and was it possible that they had continued to advance?

Zack theorized that the ceramic artifact on the Savitar that Craig was to examine would give them a clue as to where. The possibility of their continuation was a much more mysterious and fanciful situation.

He commented that it was hard for him to fathom two-hundred-twenty million years of survival when the human race had only now achieved a few thousand years.

He asked if they still existed and continued to advance, why had they not returned.

Zack commented that more than likely their time had passed.

Tears again came to Janet. She had a different feeling. She was still affected by the fact that some Martian had led the remains of the Martian civilization through the entire solar system and to her it seemed they had gone somewhere beyond.

She felt that person would not have done so if they had not believed they would succeed.

She made a promise to herself to learn if they had indeed flourished in some other part of the Milky Way. She felt a pull that she knew she would follow until they opened the box and learned more about the brave group that survived the blackhole.

<u>Chapter 4: On Earth once More</u>

The return back up to the Sprite left all of them wanting more time to explore on the surface. This was not one of the choices they had. They instead headed for Earth. They had been granted a side trip but they were expected back so that the next flight out to the Savitar could stay on schedule.

The information they had collected on Mars was shared globally. It triggered new interest and support for the effort to explore Mars. The Sprite would be one of the ships providing that transport. The other space faring countries also planned expeditions to Mars.

Zack and Craig were pleased that they had once again energized the people of Earth.

The two of them had continued to discuss how to develop the equivalent of gravity for the spaceships already in the field and for any future vessels that would be built.

Janet threw her idea into the ring. She suggested that the current ships have a long cable similar to those on the Savitar going between the nine G and one G levels attached to their roof. This cable could go out to a counterweight and at the center would be the propulsion engine. The engine of the current ship would provide rotational speed to create the equivalent of one G while the center engine would provide the drive through space. The counterweight could be fuel or water or any other weight that made sense.

Captain Moffet laughed and joked that Janet must have attended a much better Engineering College than either Zack or Craig. Her degree seemed to provide the learning and the ideas that seemed of late to have been lacking in previous discussions.

Both Zack and Craig agreed. They had overlooked a simple design and had been lost in the forest of complexity.

Zack immediately suggested this idea to Ben Samualson, the NASA director.

The response was an excited affirmative and a promise to immediately work on implementing the concept.

They had all the materials necessary to make it happen for the Sprite on her arrival.

The Sprites' arrival and their ride down on one of the new shuttles seemed to set the stage for their visit.

The President greeted them personally. A long red carpet was rolled out to several waiting limos.

The news media had been held back but they shouted questions.

Zack stopped for a minute and walked over so he could address them.

He shared the fact that two hundred million years before humans populated the Earth sentient beings had arisen on Mars. Thes beings had traveled the solar system during the age of the dinosaur two hundred million years ago.

The blackhole that his team had captured and moved out Earth's way gave humans the opportunity to continue their development whereas the Martians had to flee from the black hole and travel through the solar system and to finally leave.

Humankind needed to recognize the Earth as the common home for all of the human population. He made the point that every person on the Earth was precious and should be treated as such.

Zack turned and slowly followed the President.

Craig commented to the President, who was a personal friend that he was still having to deal with the idealist student that he had mentored.

"Are you referring to that person that the Savitar crew now calls a President," Dan commented. "I plan to come out and run against him for the next Savitar election," Dan continued as the led the way.

The limo took them to their hotel. There they were met by Bill Masterson, FBI director and Zack's friend and previously Janet's top boss.

After customary greetings and hellos, he jokingly asked if Janet had come back to accept his job promotion offer.

Fred, Janet's previous direct boss, now in the position that had previously been offered to her, cried foul. He claimed to have just bought a new house because of his promotion.

Janet joked back that she had only returned because she had heard that Bill had promised her another vacation in Hawaii.

Bill was there to introduce the bodyguards being assigned to the four of them for the duration of their visit and who he had personally selected. Two were women and two were men.

Zack thanked Bill and pointed out that his greatest protector was with him and would be at his side for the entire visit.

Bill agreed but pointed out that this was Janet's vacation and that he had once again arranged for her to enjoy the same villa that she had enjoyed on her previous visit to Maui and while there both of them would have round-the-clock bodyguards.

Bill then let them know that his parents and his sister were already in Washington and in their hotel suite. They were staying in one of the larger rooms. Their stay was a huge plug for the hotel, and the hotel management was eager to please.

Zack led Janet onto the elevator. The attendant pressed the button to the top-level residential suite.

Craig and Emily were going to stay in the same suite.

Madillen, his sister, rushed forward and gave Zack and Janet a hug. Zack's mother and father both were beaming and gave Zack a hugs as well.

Marian gave Janet a hug and thanked her for keeping her son in one piece and alive. She had learned of the assassination attempts and their failures. She jokingly asked if it had been worth it.

Janet replied that she was planning to marry him for the second time when they all went to Maui.

Madillen announced that she was planning to get married on the upcoming trip to Hawaii as well.

The announcement surprised everyone. She laughed and said she had proposed to her boyfriend. She was tired of waiting for his proposal and she was not going to miss the chance of having Janet be her maid of honor and her brother be the best man.

Besides, she pointed out that Zack had offered to pick up all expenses. He was now a rich President, and she was going to leverage the situation.

Janet knew that Zack had offered to pay everyone's way to Maui. She also knew that the only money the two of them had was the money that they had left in trust accounts held in their bank on Earth. And she knew that Zack was getting no pay as the first President of the Savitar.

She chose to reinforce Madillen's position. She asked Zack if he had reserved a private plane to take them all to Maui in fashion. She went on to say that after all a President should have his own private jet.

Zack laughed. He and Janet had already talked through this subject, but he chose to act surprised.

He let out a moan and claimed to have forgotten the trip to Maui.

Craig and Emily had been in on the preparation for Hawaii and understood and were enjoying the family teasing and joking that was going on.

Emily said in a surprised voice that she thought they were all going to Rio for their vacation.

Bill knew when it was time to leave. He reminded everyone that the formal Presidential dinner would be on the following evening.

He made the point that he knew space-faring people seldom carried their tuxes with them and that a tailor with all the proper tuxedoes and accruements would be making sure everyone was properly dressed.

He shared that like last time, his wife had arranged getting Janet's dress and jewelry. He suggested that Emily call the same place and order her outfit because they had been warned to expect that call.

He then pointed to the bodyguards and said that they should not forget their presence.

Zack thanked him as he left.

The family agreed that everyone should get situated in their rooms and then they would meet in the private dining room to enjoy dinner together.

Marian, Madillen sat across from Janet and Emily and accosted them with a barrage of questions about the journey out to the black hole and life aboard the Savitar. They specifically asked Emily if she had gotten over her concern about having left Earth.

Emily smiled and replied that she had never envisioned the full and exiting life she was living on the Savitar.

Zack asked his father whether they should do some crabbing. They decided that it would be worth an evening, but they would cook the crabs while still on the beach.

The next day was a free day. One part of the group went shopping.

Zack and Craig decided to visit the team that was now assigned to the Path Finder program and meet with them personally. They figured that doing so in person would create a closer working partnership. When they arrived they found that their Path Finder members had brought their families in so they could meet the two of them. It was good that neither had a specific work agenda in mind.

Later they met briefly with the team of specialists that were working on how to get the information in the ceramic box without the need to open it.

In both cases they knew they were investing in establishing a closer working relationship and no real work got done.

They returned to the hotel to get ready for the dinner at the White House.

The dinner was superb and the attention to them was overwhelming. Zack was glad that the press was limited to the few top organizations, and they were kept along the periphery of the room and had a brief question time at the beginning.

The highlight of the dinner party was a private meeting he held with them.

Zack thanked the president for all his support.

The President turned that around and thanked Zack for giving him a second term in office. He then voiced his desire to come out and travel with the Savitar. He had talked it over with his wife and the two of them thought it was a novel idea to set up his Presidential Library on the Savitar.

He then added after Zack's second term as President of the Savitar, he planned to run for President again but this time as the president of the Switzerland of Space.

Bram smiled and replied that he would be pleased to have his friend Dan come up to the Savitar and run for President. He added that he was sure that he would make a good President for the Savitar.

He made the point that he personally did not plan to run for a second term.

The dinner ended with a final set of questions from the press and then they returned to the hotel.

The trip to Hawaii followed two days later. Zack had arranged for a jet to transport everyone. The entire cabin was a first-class design that featured seats that became full beds.

Madillen kept telling her future husband that if he just applied himself, he too, like her brother, would be able to afford such luxury.

Zack overheard the comment and added, "Yes but you will have to find your own black hole to capture. I am not sharing mine."

There were two simultaneous weddings on the beach. Madillen was in a full white gown and was following a traditional wedding schedule.

Janet and Zack wore matching Maui t-shirts and white docker shorts. Zack had arranged for an emerald bracelet with a miniature Savitar hanging on it instead of another wedding band. This again surprised Janet since she did not know when Zack had found the time to commission the bracelet.

She knew that Zack wore no jewelry. She had purchased a recording of "Savitar Sings" as her wedding gift.

The press, out in full, was kept a decent distance away but Janet knew that the pictures of the wedding would get international attention.

Madillen and her new spouse chose to go back to the home they were all staying in. Madillen wanted to change and get ready for the reception.

Half of the press followed them.

Janet took Zack's hand and led him along the water's edge for a walk. She knew that she had been granted her wish. She was walking with her soul mate along one of the most beautiful beaches in the world. She could think of nothing better.

Her only distraction was the bevy of cameras and news announcers that followed them. She was pleased that their bodyguards successfully kept them a decent distance away.

She took Zack to the black lava rock where she showed him the crabs and fish and shared her thoughts about how their world was a microcosm of the one that people on Earth seemed to live.

Then she led him back to where the public shower area and was surprised to meet the same person that washed the sand back to the beach. It was clear to her that the flowers he was holding were for her.

He commented that he had followed her travels as best he could and that he wanted to thank her for helping save the world.

Janet thanked him and introduced Zack to him.

He shared how impressed he was with the fact that she had captured the person who had thought up the idea of moving a blackhole. He asked whether it had been a hard thing for her to.

Janet laughed and said that indeed she had to save him so many times that she wondered when if ever he would propose.

Janet invited him to dinner. He thanked her but politely declined.

A day later, she and everyone but Madillen and her husband boarded the plane and flew back to Washington. The two of them were going to spend another week in Hawaii.

The rest of them spent one day in Washington and then they went on to Florida.

Zack commented that he was suffering the Milton syndrome and received a pat on the back from Craig and a ditto from Janet.

His mother asked what the Milton syndrome was all about. She laughed at the explanation that it implied getting overwhelmed by having too much space. It was a condition given this name on the Savitar because Zack had created so much more space for everyone to enjoy that they had voiced the concern about feeling vulnerable.

That evening Zack and his entire family went crabbing. The surprise was the arrival of a bushel of live crab that had been sent by the President. A few crab were caught and eaten but the bushel allowed more time to be spent sipping a beer and getting the meat from the crabs that were boiled Cajun style.

The last night before blastoff was spent at the Milton home. A backyard barbeque followed by rhubarb-strawberry pie and coffee on the enclosed porch once again re-reinforced to Janet the great family Zack had.

Zack was pleased that this time, his last moments on Earth were spent with his parents. He had felt guilty on his previous departure because of the security issues, he had not arranged to see them during the last few days.

Chapter 5: Return

The redesign of the Sprite to having gravity was immediately embraced by everyone. The new configuration that Janet had suggested had been augmented with rocket engines of the Indian design and provided a faster return to the Savitar.

Additionally, there were two spheres on opposite ends of a two-hundred-mile cable. The Sprite was on another cable. An engine on what was now the outside of the Sprite and a similar engines on the spheres were used to steer. The Sprite engines provided the rotational thrust.

Zack complimented Janet on her simple design.

Janet looked at the engineering drawings and gave a small laugh. She commented that she had no idea that the final configuration would look or operate in the manner that it did.

She commented that she was pleased that she had helped to make a design breakthrough and was happy that she would be traveling with the feeling of one G versus being weightless and nauseous.

The force of gravity made the trip out toward the Savitar much more pleasant than their trip had been to Mars and to Earth.

Zack was excited about this progress and planned to have all the ships assigned to the Savitar modified.

As the Sprite approached the Savitar, Captain Moffet pointed out the similar modification of the Rama and then he pointed out that all the space shuttles had similar designed systems.

He commented that the Rama had three spheres and wondered what that implied. When questioned, Captain Enrico of the Savitar replied that the additional spheres provided additional storage space. The desire to extract fuel from the moon Titan led to the implementation of additional storage.

Conrad Zepf's engineering team and the Boss teamed up and fabricated the entire system in record time as soon as they had received the drawings.

Zack was pleased with Enrico's initiative in improving the Rama. This would greatly help in making the trip much more enjoyable when they went out to study the Titan Martian colony.

The work of filling in another pentagon with the ceramic Buckie balls was in its final stages. The ceramic decking was being laid as fast as the Buckie structure went in place.

What amazed both Zack and Craig, was that the enclosure for the pentagon and structure to house the equipment they were bringing from Earth to facilitate the examination of the Martian ceramic box was ready.

Lars, "the boss," commented that Victor had all of his people activated to deliver the power. Gregor had activated his logistics folks and had provided every bit of material that the Savitar had in stock. Paulo had unleashed his welders to assemble whatever needed to be welded.

He and Sampson had utilized every willing body to get the pentagon platform ready. He said that every person on the Savitar wanted to find out what was in the ceramic box and almost every one of them had volunteered their spare time to get the pentagon done.

The specialists that had come out with the equipment worked with Lars, the "Boss", to get it positioned and powered up. They commented that they had never experienced a structure so amazingly clean.

The clean room was built and powered up.

Zack and Craig watched as the clean room team sterilized, and moved the box to an examination "cart". This was much more of what Zack would have called a robot. The cart could pick up the box and extent it out. This allowed the box to be held and moved into various examination units.

Zack made the comment that he should leave more often but he was afraid to be gone because the Savitar would leap forward in his absence and he would be left behind.

For the next three weeks Craig was closely involved with the equipment, the linguistics and other specialists setting up the equipment and going over the process by which the box would be examined.

Janet and Susan and the linguistic specialists that had come out to the Savitar and those back on Earth were pouring over the ceramic inscription that had been found on Titan and the plaque that had been found on Mars. It became clear to them that they needed a Rosetta stone that would give them the secret of all the symbols they were working with.

They were now eager to see what was inside of the ceramic box.

Zack sympathized with the frustration that Janet was experiencing. On his return he had been undated in the various "critical" governmental decisions that had been waiting for him to finalize. The amount of dull, management work overwhelmed him and made him wish for a quick end to his term as President.

It was clear to him that he would be a one term President of the Savitar. He was an investigator, an inventor, a searcher. He was not cut out to manage the affairs of state. His decision was a relief and reduced the tensions that seemed to have arisen.

He sent out a private message to Dan that he should come out to the Savitar when his term as US president was over. The Savitar would need a capable new President in the very near future.

Lisa and her team had waited until the garden areas and the new green house on the ceramic pentagon was completed, then they populated the new facility with the most exotic plants they had.

They did not abandon their original gardens that had been initially used on their way out to the blackhole. They were refurbished and used as additional starter facilities. These original gardens became as important as the newer larger ones.

They had spent a lot of time deciding on what to plant in the park. They ended up taking a few plants from each of the other five pentagons.

Lisa was especially impressed with the ability for the personnel reclaiming materials from space to provide the "dirt" for the park.

She was constantly sending treats to the personnel doing the recovery and material separation. She wanted them to know how much their work mattered.

She and Enrico hosted Zack, Susan, Craig, and Emily for a picnic in the new park. The team working in the new green house and who would move out to the new pentagon when the living facilities were ready, provided the grilling and preparation of the food. It was all "local" to that pentagon.

The picnic triggered the idea to have an open house for the entire Savitar population.

Zack asked Conrad Zepf to have his organization schedule and manage an open house. It would have music, food, and structured tours. Each of the other pentagons was to be asked to provide help and provide some part of the food for the picnic.

Zack was especially impressed with the clean room building.

It had three levels of "cleanliness." The box could be seen from the first top level.

The first level required that a gown to cover the clothes, hair net to cover the hair and beard and shoe covering be used. No jewelry watch or rings could be worn. To get to the second level, people had to shower and change clothes and undergo ultraviolet light treatment. From this level via observation windows, they could look into and observe what was happening at the third cleanliness location in greater detail.

The second level was where the cameras, voice recorders and all the computer hardware that supported the special equipment at the next level was located. It was the brain center.

To enter the final level a person had to take another shower. This shower was a chemical disinfectant mist that took fifteen minutes. Then there was a final light irradiation treatment step.

It took almost an hour to get to the cleanest level.

Zack made it clear that the open house tour would be limited to the first level.

Craig let everyone know that he was going to go full speed ahead with his examination of the box. He and his team of specialists had developed a plan that would consume them for almost a year before they would even consider opening the ceramic chest.

This plan had been reviewed with everyone on the Savitar and their team members on Earth. Duplicate and separate analysis would be done by each location and then reviewed, and conclusions aligned.

The goal was understanding all they could without taking the chance of losing the precious information they were certain was inside.

Craig asked if there were any concerns.

Zack asked if the linguistic specialists were part of the planning effort.

Susan reassured him that she and Janet had been part of the planning effort. She went on to say that the linguistic team had a small overlap with the box investigative team, but it was utilizing every resource both on the Savitar and on Earth as well.

The desire of the world to learn what was in the box and to break the linguistic barrier was a major driving force. Everything seemed to the common person to be moving too slow, and the media wanted to know why more resources were not being used to speed up the process. They found it hard to believe that every resource was being used.

Zack, in his position as President of the Savitar had been pressured by the media to answer why the box was being held captive on the Savitar instead of being sent to Earth for examination.

He took the time to share the fact that the box would remain on the Savitar for as long as it took to learn about it but that all the resources of Earth were being utilized. It was going as fast as was humanly possible. He added that whatever they learned would be shared with Earth's population.

He shared the date when the team on the Savitar would begin its active look into the ceramic box.

Craig woke up to the smell of breakfast. He knew that Emily was fixing blueberry pancakes that he looked forward to smothering in some syrup that had been made on the Savitar, two eggs and bacon that had been brought out on their return from Earth.

She had invited Zack, Janet, Mary, and Jeff over as well.

Emily knew that it was the day when Craig and his group were going to look into the box with the CT scanner and everyone would get their first look as to what was inside.

She, Zack, Mary, and Jeff along with many other Savitar leaders would be standing in the second level clean area. They would be able to look at the box and on a large screen they would be able to see its contents.

Janet and Craig were the only two in their group that would be able to touch the box.

Confluence

Zack at Craig's urging had kept the first day of examination a secret from the general population of both the Savitar and Earth. He wanted a period of time to examine the contents with only his team and the linguistics team. He then planned to step back and spend time with the initial new knowledge and spend time on interpreting and understanding what had been learned.

The analysis team would continue to carry out a series of non-invasive tests.

It took most of the morning to get everyone into position. Everyone waited patiently as Janet, Craig and two specialists made their way into the final level.

Zack was sitting in the second cleanliness level exchanging messages with Janet. The observation level had a big screen, bottled water and comfortable formed chairs made of ceramic.

He, Emily, Mary, and Jeff were the only ones that had chosen to go to the bother of going through to the second level.

The Savitar Extended Leadership team would all observe from the forward command center via computer connection.

Lars and Sampson and some of their team were at level one. At that level they could enjoy coffee and other snacks. They figured going farther diminished their comfort level.

They were all eager to get their first glimpse.

The equipment to view the inside of the Martian ceramic box was positioned and made ready.

Craig stood and looked at the camera. He commented that there should be music, a drum roll and a speech to expound on the significance of this moment.

He made the point that he had not prepared any of that and together they would all see the contents at the same time.

Janet had spent more than two hours making it through the third cleanliness level. She waited patiently for Craig to complete the cleansing process. The body suit she wore left little to the imagination. It was designed to seal the human body and it was skintight and transparent. She had insisted on a dark pair of shorts and matching halter top be imprinted on the body suit. This was made of a similar material to the body suit. It was made to be worn similar to any such shorts and halter top. This was a design that had been adopted for both sexes. Her female counterparts thanked her for adding these accruements to what initially had been just the clear body suit.

She wondered if the three levels of cleanliness were necessary. If the time estimate of the age of the box, based on the time for the solar system to make one revolution around the Milky Way was right, then the box would have been sitting on the anchor for two-hundred-million years. It had been exposed to the toxic Titan atmosphere all that time.

It had survived with a smooth shiny exterior. The seam around the lid was visible only under the scrutiny of a one-hundred power microscope. It was the most sophisticated seal that anyone on Earth had ever seen.

She did not think the box needed any of the security that had been taken. She felt this level of precaution would be reasonable when the box was to be opened. She was not convinced that she would still be around when the time came to open the ceramic chest.

The examination equipment was positioned.

Craig made his brief announcement.

He stood for a minute looking at the box. He was more nervous at this moment than he had ever been. The last time had been at the moment when he had put the ring on Emily's finger and promised until death and for better or for worse.

He kept his eyes closed until he heard Emily shout out, "Oh, my god, it is beautiful."

He looked at the image the CT system had compiled from the thousands of slices it had taken of the interior of the box.

There was a semi-clear almost translucent crystalline cube. Emily commented that the cube was absolutely stunning as it shimmered on the screen.

There were etchings on a ceramic plate that depicted what Craig took to be the Martians.

The most startling discovery was the position sketch of the solar system. It clearly depicted nine planets! The Martians had discovered all of them.

There was a second white cube with forty symbols and what seemed to be a numbering system based on eight. He was sure the mathematicians would have a field day with that.

The final diagram depicted what could only be the journey the Martians had taken as they traveled through the solar system.

There was writing on the lid, but it would need to be turned around. The system scan had the writing in reverse.

Janet was lightheaded. She sat down. She identified the glowing ceramic cube as the Rosetta stone.

Craig commented on the fact that they would be able to establish the time when the Martians had existed by the position of the stars shown in the solar system diagram.

Silence descended as everyone took in the wealth of learning that this first glimpse had given them.

Craig knew that there would be good days like they were now experiencing and then there would be very frustrating ones when nothing seemed to go the way they hoped.

Zack kept looking at the screen. He realized that he had seen the cube before. It was Déjà vu. He was certain he had seen it before.

He could not talk. His voice failed him. He was in a state of shock. He could not make the leap to the fact that he had seen the cube before.

He whispered to Emily that he had seen the crystal cube before.

Emily in turn stood up and shouted that Zack had seen the cube before.

For a full minute, everyone was silent.

Finally, Janet quietly asked Zack if he was going to share with the rest of them where he had seen it before.

Zack apologized for his silence, shook his head and then he said seeing the cube in the box had been one of the greatest shocks in his life and he had gone blank, but it had finally come to him where he had seen the crystalline cube.

He had seen it when he visited Harvard when he was trying to decide on the school he planned to go to.

The crystal he had seen was damaged but was still in one piece. It was on either the fifth or sixth floor of the Peabody Museum of Archaeology and Ethnology. It was under glass on a long table full of interesting rocks from all over the world. As best as he could remember that crystal had been found in a diamond mine in Central Africa.

Craig made the snide comment that not remembering the floor or where the crystal was located would cost them a lot of time and that he thought Zack could do much better.

Emily gave Zack a hug and told him not to listen to her flaky, outrageous husband.

Janet suggested they get the President to send out a team to secure the crystal that Zack had seen before the information leaked out.

<u>Chapter 6: The View</u>

Zack turned and left the viewing room and placed a secure call to President Lansing with the request. He decided he would go out to the park to place the call. He needed the time to organize his request and to think through how the cube in Boston could be used to help the effort to learn about the Martians. He also wondered about the origin of the cube.

He stood outside for a long time and envisioned the Martian ship hovering over Earth and launching an information cube down onto the surface of Pangea. He thought about the fact that the Martians were so close physically but that on an individual level they could never survive physically on Earth. The gravitational force was a barrier that could not be overcome. Their bodies were not strong enough to survive Earth's gravity.

They had visited and had left their knowledge knowing that intelligence would arise. They could not have imagined that it would be two hundred million years in the future.

A few hours later his call to the President, the Peabody Museum of Archaeology and Ethnology was surrounded by a host of FBI cars and everyone inside detained. One of Janet's Earth side team members was with them and led the way to the floor where the various stones were on display. It turned out it was on the fifth floor.

The cube now stood out like a sore thumb. How it had been mistaken as a beautiful but simple crystalline stone would be discussed for years to come.

The crystal was extensively photographed and then put into a sterile case and whisked away.

Janet once again wondered about the need for a sterile case. The crystal had been handled and then been on display for years and exposed to the atmosphere.

The caravan of eight vehicles made their way to where the crystal would be kept.

The pictures sent up to the Savitar confirmed that the crystal on Earth was the same design as the one in the ceramic box.

Plans were made to analyze the crystal.

Janet immediately left level three and met her team in their new offices that were part of the new clean room building. This was located on the first level.

She had worked with the designers to ensure the desks, chairs and extra-large screens were part of each person's work area.

She had all of her team focus on the ceramic cube that seemed to show a forty-character based alphabet and an eight-digit numbering system.

She was eager for the team to put their minds into understanding and interpreting the inscriptions they had found on the giant anchor on Titan, the inscriptions on the ceramic box lid, and the inscription on the plague they had recovered on Mars.

She and the team on the Savitar would focus on the anchor inscription and the box lid inscription. The part of the team on Earth would focus on the inscription on the Martian plaque.

The Earth was far enough away that communication was in the form of full messages. This made teamwork a little harder, but Janet insisted that the team keep itself functioning as one. They had separate tasks, but they had one common goal.

Craig almost as quickly had his team focused on trying to understand how to read the crystal cube recovered on Earth. The challenge facing his team was that they would need to figure out how to extract information from the crystal cube of which they had no clue as to this work.

He believed that the ability to touch and examine the damaged crystal would lead to a breakthrough in their ability to gain access to the cube sealed in the ceramic chest.

Progress was slow. The team had been trying almost every combination of light frequencies they could think of. What type of light was the frustrating question that seemed to elude them.

Emily listened to Craig's and Zack's dinner discussion about the light frequency issue.

She looked at Janet commented that if she were leaving a cube that needed light for it to function and the expectation was that some other civilization would find and try to make it function, she would make sure it operated on the light coming from the sun.

The room fell into a long thunderous silence.

Emily realized that everyone was staring at her. She put up her hands and said she surrendered.

Janet stood up, went to where Emily was sitting and gave her a hug.

She looked at Craig and complemented his spouse for giving them the best direction that anyone had given them so far. She made the point that not only was Emily a renowned Solar Chef, but she was also the best Solar sleuth that she knew. She asked if anyone wanted to bet with her that Emily had figured out the right answer.

The message to Earth was sent out suggesting streaming in the sunlight and directing it to the crystal. By the following morning, the team on Earth had set up the crystal to see if they could power it up using direct sunlight.

Craig's reaction when he heard the crystal did indeed function by utilizing sunlight was to do a jig.

The Earth part of the team focused the light at various crystalline junctions and were rewarded with a stream of light and black bars and also light and black dashes and light and black dots. The output depended on the crystalline junction that the sunlight hit.

Craig approached Janet and asked how her team was doing in learning what the mathematics of the Martians might be and what the alphabet might be.

He needed the help of the linguistics team to decipher the dots, dashes and other information being generated by the crystal.

Janet initially thought that she and her team would be able to decipher the information on the ceramic cube, but it had been more than two weeks and the team had not made the breakthrough she thought would happen quickly.

Zack was standing in the linguistic team room looking at the pictures of the cube. He counted the eight inside surface photographs that had been posted and asked where the ninth one happened to be.

The team made up of Susan, Mitch, Elena, Adinath, Conrad and Samuel all fell silent. They had been so focused on deciphering that they all had missed the fact that one side of the box was missing.

Janet looked at Craig and asked where the ninth side of the cube might be.

Craig commented that no picture had been taken of that side. He said the ninth side was the bottom side of the cube. The scanner was on the top side of the chest. No picture had been taken of it.

He made a call to the imaging team to turn the box over and scan it in that position.

That afternoon, the translation team had additional information with which to work.

Janet now felt they were working with a full deck and would soon make the breakthrough that everyone was waiting for.

Craig was embarrassed about not having scanned the ceramic box from the bottom. When the scan from the bottom was done the team had a view of the white ceramic cube bottom. It also had the writing on the lid in forward fashion. The other surprise was that the crystalline cube seemed to have slots on the bottom as if there should be something attached.

Janet and her team looked at the picture of the engraving on the massive space anchor on Titan. They worked for almost a week and then the breakthrough that they had worked so hard to make happen, happened.

They were able to decipher the writing that was inscribed on the anchor on Titan.

The following morning, Janet held up the red card in the leadership meeting that signaled she had something to share.

Confluence

She quietly but emotionally read what had been translated.

<u>Our Song, So Bittersweet</u>

From Ancient roots

From times now past,

We on this journey,

The few,

The last.

We sing a song.

In memory,

To all that came before us,

To we those remaining few.

It is a sad song.

There are no tears.

There is no laughter.

There is no one left behind.

We ten thousand are the last.

Our time here is past.

Our future is out, out into the vast,

The vast expanse,

Of space and time.

Janet commented that she thought it as a poem written to the Martian spirits being left behind in this solar system. It was a sad poem that brought tears to her and followed her each day.

Janet had put her foot on Mars. She had seen the sterile remains. She had seen the thousands of bodies. She knew the scientists from Earth were estimating the of the number of Martians that had been eliminated by the planet's interaction with the blackhole was in excess of one billion.

Earth now had twelve billion humans.

She though how lucky Earth had been to have had someone like Zack to keep Earth from having suffered Mars' fate.

Her white knight was Earth's white knight.

Craig did not get the breakthrough help he needed to decipher the dots and dashes that were being gathered by his team. He had hoped the linguistics team would see something. He was working with a damaged cube back on Earth and wondered if he was getting useful information.

It was Enrico who posed the question as to whether a dash was about something visual like pictures or art. Perhaps a dot indicated something that could be heard. The combinations of dots and dashes were integrated information such as books with pictures.

Craig acknowledged that the logic made sense, but the output was a jumble of all of it at once.

Zack asked if the slots existed on the crystalline cube that the Earth was working with.

Craig replied that it was on the deformed side of the cube on Earth and there were no slots.

Zack looked at the cube inside the ceramic box.

He wondered out loud whether technology would let them shine light into the cube in the box and retrieve what was coming out the slots on the bottom.

Conrad Zepf replied that there might be a way to create a laser beam using the sun's light spectrum and focus it on specific crystal nodes.

An output reader would look at the light coming out of the cube slots and register the output.

The Savitar laser team had spent a year experimenting the capabilities of laser technology. Everyone agreed that they might be of help.

Conrad agreed to contact the leader of the team.

Craig thanked him and asked that the team come to the lab. He would provide any equipment they wanted.

Meanwhile he sent the current information to the Janet.

Janet, Susan, and Mary were enjoying a lunch prepared by a group of Emily's chef students. They were discussing how they might use their breakthrough to decipher what they had been given.

Emily sat down to listen to the discussion about the "Data" that Craig had sent to the linguistic team.

Emily looked at the team and suggested that the dots might actually be pot pies. Was there a way that the dots could be expanded and looked at? Each dot like a pot pie might have the goodies inside.

Janet asked if Emily wanted to join the linguistic team. Janet was sure that an exploded view of the dots would yield new learning.

Emily politely declined and asked if her students had prepared a good lunch.

Janet, Susan, and Mary rode the tube back to the ceramic pentagon. They called Craig and asked him whether there was a way to greatly expand the dots.

When they arrived at what had been named the Ceramic Castle, they were met by an excited Craig. He had taken just one dot and made it the size of a watermelon. The interior was full of visuals and text.

Craig decided that he would join the linguistic team. He wanted to start developing his understanding of the Martians.

Zack had the same desire. He figured that the current location of the Savitar was near where the Martian had departed the solar system.

He had calculated the speed they might have achieved in the early spaceships. He anticipated that the Martians had the ability to accelerate and travel close to half the speed of light, that he and the Savitar had achieved on the way out to the blackhole.

He assigned a team of observers to scan the skies out equivalent to four to five hundred years of travel at that speed.

He wanted to know if there was a solar system or spot in the Milky Way that might attract the Martians. More than two-hundred-million years had passed since the Martians had left. If the Martians had survived, Zack wondered if they would still exist, and would they still remember their roots?

A week later Zack's observer team reported that they had found only one potential location. It was currently about three-hundred years from the Solar system.

Finding a location that fit so well with the travel limitations that Zack had specified excited him.

He called a meeting of all the people studying the ceramic box and proposed sending a message at light speed using the breakthrough technology the laser team had just unveiled.

The team on Earth was surprised and startled by the meeting. It was not Zack's proposal but the fact that he had chosen the meeting as the way to share the laser communication breakthrough.

It had not dawned on them how smoothly the meeting had proceeded until Zack had pointed it out. They had not noticed it because their response was being broadcast on the normal radio frequencies.

The Savitar team had a breakthrough with their laser of being able to read normal communication frequencies for both radio and video broadcasts via the ripples created in the laser stream traveling at light speed. This allowed the Savitar to get the immediate responses of their Earth side participants.

Zack agreed that the Savitar would share this technology with Earth as soon as the development team completed their work on reducing the required electrical power draw. He shared that it currently needed the power only a blackhole could provide.

Meanwhile the team would use the Savitar's blackhole to continue the refinement of the communication laser.

Zack proposed that a message be sent out to the most probable location where the Martians may have gone.

Everyone agreed with Zack's communication idea, but everyone wanted to participate in what the message would transmit.

Zack got agreement that the linguistic team would draft the content of the message. Then everyone on the Martian research effort would have input to what was sent

Privately he had shared the breakthrough with Craig and had asked him as the US ambassador to the Savitar to communicate to President Lansing that the laser was so powerful that it could easily become a weapon of war. Zack suggested that an agreement similar to the historic global Nuclear agreement be negotiated before sharing the technology.

Confluence

The power of the laser would manifest itself in the ability to establish a system that would greatly enhance the relationship between the Earth, the Savitar and the first intelligent beings of the Solar System.

Ron Mueller

Chapter 7: Break Through

The damaged cube on Earth was yielding a significant amount of information. The breakthrough in being able to explode the dots and then extract information made a significant difference. However, the information being extracted though understandable seemed to be in random order.

There was a desire to see how light could be directed into the cube in a controlled manner.

Bram had suggested that they try to send light into the cube in the ceramic box.

Bram thought that perhaps the laser team that had developed a tremendous amount of knowledge on how to generate and control light might be of help.

The laser team on the Savitar had eagerly joined the effort and had been allocated one of the newly completed labs on the newly finished pentagon. They set up their equipment and went to work with Craig's team to see if they could figure out how to send light into the cube in the ceramic box.

Craig had provided the laser team with all the information at hand. Conrad had joined the laser team and had them working around the clock.

It was clear to Craig that Zack's idea of utilizing the cube inside the ceramic box had merit, and his team went to work to develop a way to send in sunlight and a means to extract the light with the information being sent out. He was not sure how long the development would take.

He realized that the information being collected from the damaged cube on Earth was random in nature, but it might provide a means to get a better understanding of the Martians.

The random information being extracted from the damaged crystalline cube on Earth was not as random as initially anticipated. The extraction logic followed the crystalline structure from the outer edge and went clockwise around. Each node on each crystal followed the same pattern around the crystal nodes.

The information seemed to be following a connected timeline thread.

Janet and her research team were overwhelmed.

Her IT support group had devised an initial translation software that accelerated the translation effort. This was a breakthrough and it greatly enhanced the speed with which the translation was occurring.

She realized that even with the new translation software being used by a team of translators and a video editing and vocal overlay staff providing around the cloak support, the work ahead would take many years.

The first piece of translation of the inscription on the plaque she had found came up from Earth. It was another tear-jerker.

She sat and cried as she put it in context as she pictured the events that she imagined had occurred.

The deciphered presentation provided several distinctive point about the Martians. They came in three colors.

They stood erect and had feet similar to a squirrel's feet.

Their voice frequencies were in a higher frequency range than human hearing ability.

They had four digits on each hand. A digit equivalent to the human thumb and three equivalent to the fingers made up each hand. It appeared the thumb was move versatile than the human one.

The team recovered a voice recording. The audio was adjusted so the soprano had the equivalent range of the best Earth soprano. The male singer had his range adjusted to that of the best baritone range.

Then after the mastering, Janet and her team listened to what everyone took to be a live performance. The soprano's haunting melody and words seemed to trace the crawl from the sea, the lunge forward with the first breath of air, the burning rays of day, the healing power of the night, and the life-giving cover of the caves.

Janet realized that her team was a captivated audience half out of their seats and swaying with every word. She smiled when she realized she was also half out of her seat and swaying like her team.

Janet sensed that the words carried the Martian audience through the path, the maze, and the pain of their history. She took the deep thundering drums to be a meteor's impact on the planet. It was accompanied by the deep voice of an instrument that sounded like a bassoon.

She imagined the cracking of the planet's mantle and dramatic altering of the magnetic field as she took in the piercing howls of pain.

She and her team listened as a thunderous voice rose and went on to tell how nature ignored the formidable damage and miraculously created and expanded life in the incredibly deep water filled canyons that the impact had created. These deep canyons were made by the impact of a huge asteroid and the splitting of the planet's mantle. Most of the planet's water flowed into these canyons but much of the water was lost into space.

The damage went deep into the core and dramatically altered the magnetic field. The sun's unimpeded radiation killed all in its path. From the beginning the night and shadow became the nurturer and the sun's unfiltered rays the extinguisher of life.

The ravaged atmosphere was too shallow and the distorted magnetic field too weak to shield the planet from the stream of sterilizing radiation flowing out from the sun.

Life evolved by embracing the night and by keeping to the depths of the radiation shielding canyons.

Life slowly, in millions of years, achieved sentience and intelligence.

Janet knew that this was a Martian survival celebration and all in attendance breathed the words, leaned slowly forward and then back in unison with the singer in the spotlight.

The singer's shadowed eyes juxtaposed against the brightness of the light signified the battle between the sun and the shadow in the depth of their canyons.

Janet breathed in the story of survival, the story of life, love, and the story of death. This was an ancient story of love, of family and of hope. She felt the power of the performance as it swept over her like a tsunami of uncontrolled emotion.

Janet and her team took this as proof of Martian fortitude and the passion for life. Earth with all its faults had a similar regard and passion for life.

Janet told everyone to go to their quarters. She had reached the point that was more than she could take. The breakthrough in understanding their long-ago Martian ancestors was exhilarating but also emotionally exhausting.

At the next session Janet had the team focus on the inscription that had been on the plaque she had found on Mars.

She recalled the funeral chamber where the plaque had been found.

The plaque seemed to be a poem.

OUR TIME IS PAST

From Ancient roots
From times now past
We stay behind and we are at rest.
Our brothers and sisters, journey on.
They are alive.
They are the last.
They will remember us.
They will sing our song.
Our time is past.
They are the last.

Everyone on the team believed that the poem had been written by the was the same author as that of the poem found on the anchor and the inscription on the lid of the ceramic box.

They had several experts analyze the two and they came to the same conclusion. They were sure that the writer had been in all the locations, had great talent and must have been a leader.

Janet and her team decided the poems, the survival opera and comparable information about the Earth which seemed to be referred to as the Blue Jewel by the Martians would be the information they would put into the message to be sent to where the Martians might be. She hoped that they were still in existence.

The content of the message to the departed Martians was the center of all discussions,

Janet and her team were honing-in on the final message to be sent out toward the location that had been identified having the highest potential of contacting the Martians.

They would learn that their aim indeed would hit the target they were hoping to hit.

Chapter 8: Janet's Frustration

The information coming from the Martian crystalline cube located on the Earth kept coming in. The pattern of storage seemed to have been each layer of the crystalline structure starting from the entrance represented a layer of storage. Each juncture of the crystal represented a storage area. Each layer had a million such junctures. Each Juncture had about one hundred terabytes of storage. This meant that a cube would be able to hold many hundreds of times more information that was currently held on Earth's computers!

The realization of the massive about of information that this represented was on the one-hand a boon to the knowledge that they would eventually decipher but on the other-hand to Janet it meant she might never learn the two key things she now wanted to know.

First, she wanted to know if the Martian civilization had survived for over two-hundred and twenty million years.

And second, she desperately wanted to know who the person that had written such heart rendering poems.

She personally wanted to scream in frustration. She shared this with Zack and was surprised by his answer.

He told her that he had known from the day of her selection as his bodyguard to this moment in his life and to as far in the future as he would survive that he would always be in love with her. He had bought his diamond ring and his wedding rings before they left Earth, but he had not proposed to her until after the Savitar had successfully captured the small black hole. He did not want to worry about her emotions as he focused on making sure he could save everyone on the Savitar.

Even after she saved his life three times he had not proposed. When he knew they all had a future he finally was willing to think about "until death do us part."

He asked her to think about the Martian tragedy and think about the triumph of a small surviving band. Think of their frustration and their unbelievable struggle to survive.

He suggested she commit herself to the objective of finding them and that she would communicate with them maybe not tomorrow but in that she would communicate with them her lifetime. He suggested she be the warrior that she had shown herself to be. She had the fortitude to undertake something that she might never achieve. He predict that when she adopted that approach she would get the breakthrough she was seeking.

Janet had no reply. She gave Zack a hug and a kiss.

This was the first admonishment that he had ever verbally shared with her. It was the right thing and she committed herself to push all the learning buttons available to her.

She visited Conrad and his engineering team to see how they were progressing with developing the ability to read the undamaged cube located in the Martian ceramic box.

His response left her feeling empty. And as she was about to turn to leave a brilliant thought came to her. She asked if she could have lunch served to them by a world class Chef.

Conrad was surprised by the request. For him, the invite was out of left field, but his team were all enthused and said sure.

Janet called Emily and asked if she could arrange a special "Chef prepared meal" for the team trying to read the Martian undamaged crystalline memory cube. She stipulated that she wanted Emily to be a part of the people sitting around the table discussing the barriers to reading the information in the cube.

Emily agreed to arrange such a meal and to participate as requested. She asked if she was free to set the menu and the time length for the meal and asked when Janet wanted this event to happen.

She also asked why she should be part of those sitting at the table.

Janet responded that she would like the meal to be scheduled as soon as possible, and to last as long as possible.

She said that she wanted her to listen and ask questions when she did not understand what was being discussed.

She then asked Craig and Zack to be a part of such a meal.

She went back to Conrad and his group and shared her objective for holding the lunch meal session.

Conrad and his team asked why this discussion was being held over lunch?

Janet replied that one of the three people not on the team that would be present during the meal would provide the catalyst for the solution to the problem they all faced.

She made the point that no notes, papers, or other means of documenting would be allowed at the lunch. Everyone was to come to lunch with an open mind and then try to answer the questions that surfaced.

Janet arranged the seating in a specific pattern. Zack sat at the head of the table. Craig sat at the other end of the table. Conrad sat to the right of Zack and she sat to the left. She sat Emily in the middle on the opposite side from where she was sitting. The team was then arranged by gender. The table ended up having exactly a man to woman seating. Each person had a large name tag identifying them and the role they were in.

Zack was the Savitar President, Craig the US ambassador, Conrad was the Savitar Science Officer, she was the Linguistics team leader and Emily was the Solar System Chef.

A day later she started out the meal by introducing herself and her current objective of preparing a message to send out to the Martians. She then asked everyone at the table to introduce themselves and their current objective in the next year.

The salad was placed in front of each person as they finished their introduction. The introductions went to her left which meant that Zack was the last person to receive his salad.

Janet listened carefully as each subsequent person picked up on her theme. The exception was Emily who said that her focus was to train enough Chefs so every person on the Savitar could eat the best food in the Universe.

Janet interrupted the introductions to raise her glass of wine to make a toast to Emily as the best Chef in the Universe. After the toast she signaled the next person to continue the round of introductions.

The introductions and the toast seemed to get the lunch going. The salad was followed by a ring of shrimp placed decoratively around a large scallop smoother with a brown sauce.

After everyone was served, she asked each person on the team to describe in their own words and in words that she and Emily, neither of whom had a science or engineering degree, could understand. She warned that if it sounded like gobbly-gook to either of them, she or Emily would clink their glass with a spoon to indicate that the person should quit talking and the next person should give it a try.

The first round went rather quickly as she and Emily repeatedly clinked their glasses. When it got to Conrad and he got clinked by Emily, he asked what was next.

Janet made the point that there was one more person that had not yet been clinked. She asked Zack about his thoughts.

Zack knew that Janet had set him up. He decided not to get into the technical aspects of bending the light from various angles and having each beam strike the other in such a way as to cause a beam that would enter the cube. Then aiming it internally into the cube could be done by increasing the combination of beams.

The output would be easier to manage because the beam coming out would strike the ceramic case. The area of the case where the out-coming beam would strike could be listened to and mapped in such a manner that it could be captured. Then digital cleaning would allow for a clean signal.

He instead looked at Emily and asked her opinion of what the next steps should be.

Emily looked at Zack and replied that the main lunch course was ready to be served and the wine glasses refilled. She signaled to her staff who brought the lunch in and served in the order that had been established by Janet. Once again Zack was the last to be served.

The main course was three lamb cutlets, six spears of asparagus, a potato split into quarters with melted cheese and a sprinkle of parsley and black berries between each offering.

Emily then said that Zack should answer the question because he would have the answer of how to bend the light to create a beam that could be steered to get the needed information and he had the answer of how to sense the information coming out.

She made the point that the team on Earth had already provided the internal road map that the team on the Savitar could use to get to the last information entered by the departing Martians. She said that information would open the door to the actions they should take.

She then declared that it was time to eat and then when they finished Zack should have had enough time to think about his answer.

Janet was surprised by Emily's response. She looked at Zack and knew that Emily was right.

She decided to focus on the exquisite taste of the lamb chops and the wonderfully spiced cheese potatoes and a tangy tasting asparagus.

Once the main course was finished everyone was offered coffee or tea and gelato and a slice of pie.

Once Zack had the tea and desert served Janet waited until he was about ready to take a bite of his favorite pie and she put her hand on his wrist and said that he would get the bite only after he shared his thoughts on the question at hand.

She told him that only Emily had clinking rights.

Everyone at the lunch table stopped what they were doing and looked at Zack.

He smiled and addressed Emily. He explained to her what he would do and how he would do it. He also suggested that once the aiming of the light was mastered, the team should look for the last layer in the crystal that had information. He doubted that the crystal would be full because the estimated size of storage in the cube was at least one hundred times more information than Earth had across the entire world.

Silence ruled the table. Emily smiled and took a sip of her coffee and a bite of her pie.

Janet looked at Conrad and around at the rest of the team and asked if any of what Zack had shared made any sense. She went on to ask if it did, how long would it take to find that last layer of information?

Conrad looked at his team and after a few silent moments proposed that perhaps a couple of weeks.

Janet watched as several of the team gave positive nods.

After dinner Emily approached Janet and gave her a hug. She accused Janet of setting all of them up.

Janet agreed. She shared that she wanted to talk to the Martians in her lifetime and she had decided to utilize the best food, the best minds, and the best of Emily's ability to interpret what she understood in a fashion that caused her to make suggestions that opened knowledge doors for other people.

She thanked Emily for delivering on her part and Zack for exceeding all expectations.

Craig added it had been Zack that had made the breakthrough when the black hole was first discovered. He had repeatedly thwarted those trying to disrupt the progress of the Savitar. He had remembered a crystal that he had looked at to admire during a visit to a university that had provided the first door to the information the Martians had left to be found. Now it seemed to him that Zack had offered the solution of how to read the cube without having direct access to it.

He looked at Janet and commented that it was lucky for all of them that Zack had her around to save his life multiple times.

Janet was yet to learn of the awesome impact that Zack would lead them to in the next few years.

<u>Chapter 9: Martian Message to the Blue Jewel</u>

Conrad and his team and Craig and his team worked together to set up the equipment required to establish the light beam control into the crystal and the equipment to sense and clean the signal coming out of the crystal.

One of the team members asked if Zack was always so powerful in his thinking.

Craig replied that he and the President had both recognized Zack's keen intellect and mastery of the sciences, his amazing ability to envision a solution to a very complex problem, his ability to organize people and his ability to manage multiple events around him.

He personally had quit his University position to go into business with Zack.

The President had recognized the complete understanding of the problem that the black hole posed, Zack's solution proposal and put Zack in charge.

Both he and the President had bet their future and the world's future on Zack.

He smiled and commented that they and the world had all hit the jackpot and had won big!

Both teams quickly assembled the equipment needed to make Zack's idea come to life. The biggest barrier was to make the lenses that would precisely bend the light beams with enough accuracy and clarity to have multiple light beams come together is such a precise fashion that the result was a single larger beam that they could direct into the cube.

They enrolled the "Boss" Lars Mendelsohn to help them with getting the right group of people to make the lenses for eight beams that would be need to precisely pass through the light directed into them.

They knew that he did not have the skill to do it but that he had the skill in finding the right people to make the lenses.

Lars approached Samuel, the inventor of the nano-bots that were now used routinely by everyone on the Savitar. He asked Samuel if there was a way that the nano-bots might be used to create the kind of control that was needed.

Samuel thought about how nano-bots might be used. He replied that he did not think that they would be very useful in this specific case. He instead proposed the idea of a lens shaped in a triangle that would combine light rays and send them through to the other side of the ceramic box cover.

The cover itself would diffuse the beam into multiple color spectrum beams that once inside the box could meet at a specific angle and become one beam that could then be directed into the entrance to the cube to a specific point on the lens at the entry. This entry lens would then be controlled and enabled to send the beam to a specific layer and node inside the crystal itself.

Lars thanked him for the information and asked if he would be so kind as to take this idea to the two teams working on getting a beam inside the box and explain to them how to get the beam inside of the crystal.

Samuel eagerly went to the teams with his suggestion. By the end of the day the design for the combining lenses was developed. They were immediately fabricated from available class crystal material at hand. A test ceramic box wall was set up and the idea was tested, and the lenses modified until the combination beam could be controlled.

Conrad and his team enthusiastically worked with the light generation equipment to establish the light beam control algorithms to modulate the light in a way that changed how the beam split in the lens and how it manifested itself on the other side of the test ceramic wall.

Craig and his team observed what was being done and designed a glass light gathering plate to put on the outside of the box at the exit end of the crystal. His team played streams of light on the inside of the ceramic plate and worked at enhancing the very few photons of light that made it through the ceramic wall.

After a long week of experimentation and equipment refinement, both teams declared that they were ready to try their approach on the Martian ceramic box and the real crystalline cube.

Samuel now joined Janet, Zack, Craig, and a host of others in the first level of the clean building and watched as the equipment was set up down in the third cleanliness level where the Martian ceramic box was stored.

Janet had her team were ready to begin interpretation if the experiment worked.

The equipment was brought to power and at first there was absolute silence. It did not seem to be working. The voice of the person at the beam control computer commented that the ceramic of the Martian box seemed to be of a better quality than the ceramic that had been used to set up the control system.

She asked for a short period of time to decrease the power of the light. After decreasing the power of the light, she could be heard as she let out a breath of relief as the light inside the box split into colors and then the eight slices of light combined into a single beam that entered the crystal.

Craig's team had increased the power on their reception plate and were pleasantly surprised that the output traveling through the higher quality ceramic produced a stronger signal than had been expected. The output team had to reduce the amplification use to enhance the output from the crystal.

Janet asked her team about the reception of the signal from the Martian crystal and was pleased when she was told that the signal from the first crystal node was the same as the message from the damaged crystal node on Earth. It was the same opera scene, music, and singer from the Martian rise from the sea.

Janet then asked the operator of the light beam to see if she could find the last layer of the crystal that had information stored on it.

The operator skipped back ten layers at a time. This seemed to take a very long time as the beam was bent multiple time.

Just as Janet was going to suggest skipping back twenty or fifty layers at a time, the operator yelled that she had passed the last layer with information on her last ten-layer skip. She skipped back five layers and was back into information. She then skipped one layer at a time for two layers and was able to identify the last point of recorded data.

The light was aimed at the last node, of the last layer with data. The output team processed the output and sent it on to the translation team.

Janet watched as the node bubble was exploded and the visual came into view. Standing before her was a golden being with huge eyes, long arms and a face that would have pleased any Earth beauty queen.

She introduced herself as Nadia, leader of the ten thousand survivors of the Confluence with the black void. Her voice was similar to the soprano's. It had been brought down several octaves.

She recited the poem they had translated but her recital was an acapella song that brought tears to everyone in the room. It was filled with the pain of leaving behind those on her planet that had died. Of leaving the solar system that had given rise to her kind. Her voice was as smooth as honey, but her rendition of the message was as bitter as the place where old scorpions go to die, a place with the taste much more bitter than pure lemon juice.

She went on to show the planets of the solar system and made a point of showing Mars and then showing the travel out and then the travel back to the home world. She pointed out Earth and the travel to it. She kept referring to it as the Blue Jewel. There she pointed to a ceramic globe that was dropped to earth. It was in the section that would later form Africa but at the time there was only one land mass.

Janet bonded with Nadia and the pain she must have lived with as she guided the remnant of her people out of the solar system.

The last part of the Martian stay in the solar system was played backwards. The change in the rotating space wheel that the Martians had constructed watched in reverse seemed like they were taking their ship apart. This part seemed to have been put in as an instruction set of how to construct a ship by seeing how it had been put together.

Janet marveled at the skill with which the Martians had built their spaceship and had enlarged it to where it was five rotating wheels wide.

The team watched the rescue of the Martian colonists from Ganymede called Raulens by the Martians. Then they watched a similar rescue from Europa, known as Milan.

Again, the ship seemed to be growing smaller. It was clear that the Martians had used the materials in space to dramatically enlarge their ship. Watching progress in reverse was similar to watching a building being taken apart one piece at a time.

It was clear to Janet and everyone watching what the Martians had accomplished seemed to be the impossible.

They watched the trip back to Mars and the rotating spaceship became a fraction of the size it had been.

Then the scene changed, and the single ship went to Earth. Everyone on the Savitar was stunned as they saw the dinosaurs of the time and the giant sea creatures. They saw a grid overlay of what was now called Pangea and pictures of the huge variety of plants animals on the land, in the air and in the sea. The information from the Martian visit to earth would take someone's lifetime to study all the details.

The ship then returned to Mars.

Janet got to see Nadia's daughter that was named Hope after the last colony the Martians had established.

She saw Nadia's mother, Milan, and her father Raulens both of whom had moons named after them. She wondered why the brother Keren did not have a colony named after him. She figured one of the colony sites must not have worked out.

Janet was electrified when she saw and heard Nadia placing the plague on the door leading into the area where she, Zack and Craig had found the dust covered mounds that were later identified as bodies of Martians. Nadia clearly was the person that had been the inspiration that kept the remaining Martians alive.

Janet later shared her emotional connection to Nadia with Zack. Only the emotion she had felt when she had almost lost Zack to the depths of space had affected her so much. The difference was that the being, that elicited the overwhelming emotion, was doing it from more than two-hundred million years in the past.

Craig now had a way to extract the Martian History. The crystalline cube on the earth was providing a continuous stream of data. The crystalline cube on the Savitar provided the same information and the Martian timeline could be accurately registered.

He decided that the Earth side cube should be studied to see how the Martian technology could be reverse engineered. The storage density of the crystalline cube was greater than anything so far developed on Earth.

Janet had the team selectively sorted through the information that they had so far translated.

She freed her emotional side and let it select the elements of the message that she planned to use in preparing the draft of the message to the aliens.

Janet was now using her emotion to empower her and to provide the inspiration to see if the Martians still survived after all the time that had passed. It was a very positive emotion that gave her the energy she had felt had reached a low that she had never before experience.

She was now more connected to Nadia than ever before.

Chapter 10: The Message

The speed of information extraction from the Martian crystal went up exponentially when the aiming and extraction process was refined and was fully automated.

The opening of the Crystalline box was no longer a priority.

Craig declared that the opening would only happen in some distant future when available technology could match the technology that had enabled the sealing of the ceramic box. He postulated that the ability to make ceramic to the level that the Martians had achieved must have taken them thousands of years and have been based on the fact that they did not have the abundance of iron and had substituted ceramic for the uses that steel normally was used for on Earth.

Craig established a global organization that would manage the entire field of Martian knowledge and technology. The organization would own and manage the Martian Crystalline box. The box would remain on the Savitar in the level three clean area.

He would be involved on both the technical and political fronts associated with the new organization, but his interest was the study of the Martian encounter with the blackhole.

Zack suggested that Janet wait several days and let all the Martian information sink in before she and her team drafted the message that would be broadcast to the area that the Martian location team had selected.

She agreed with him. She took the additional step that she and her Savitar based team watched the entire trip of the Martian Spaceship Confluence in one-hour segments and then strolled through one of the six Savitar parks discussing what they had seen. She asked the Earth side members to do something similar.

The process ended up taking close to a year. It turned out that there was more Martian journey documentation then had been anticipated. Janet also came to accept the fact that several hundred million years separated her from the scenes that made her emotions surge. She accepted that she would absorb the person that she so admired.

She decided to nurture and grow her feelings and connection to Nadia and her journey of survival.

Zack was surprised at Janet's controlled approach. He asked her how she was managing her personal emotions.

Janet replied that the Martian experience would forever affect her, but she was using their experience to nurture her soul and to give it the depth that their experience generated. She said that Nadia was reaching across this immense time period and envisioning her with what she should do for the remaining time she had.

The discovery of the ancient Martian civilization had created turmoil in many of Earth's religions and in general among the lay person. She had come to the realization that her goal was to understand and create a message that would speak to both the Martians and the Earthlings.

She decided that the air, the water, the surface matter forming a ghostly swirling straw floating through space and being swallowed by the black hole and the accompanying roar of the supersonic water racing around the Martian surface would be the opening scene of the message.

Nadia's crying and her moan of pain rose up to close the opening scene.

Next came the construction of the space wheel. This was followed by showing the descent of the Martian colonists down to the surface of each of the moons Europa, ("Milan"), Ganymede, ("Raulens"), Titan, ("Hope"). The picture of the person that the colony had been named after was shown as the colonists made their descent.

Then the return to Mars and the subsequent trip to Earth was shown.

The first use of the space elevator ended with a picture of Nadia placing the plague and reading her poem in honor of the Martians that had died.

The growth of the Martian ship Confluence was shown as it proceed out toward the final point when it exited the solar system.

The retrieval of each colony was shown.

Nadia's singing and her message of hope and survival was the background throughout the visual portion of the message.

The message on the ceramic anchor on Titan, ("Hope") was accompanied by Nadia singing her farewell to those that they were leaving behind.

Janet shared the first half of her message with the Savitar leadership.

She let them know that she was now going to provide the recipients of the message with the two hundred some million-years of condensed history of the Earth and the rise of the human race.

The human side of the message began with the pictures that Nadia had taken of that early Earth and the position of the surrounding stars.

Then in an animated version of the splitting of Pangaea the super continent and its drifting to form the Americas, Europe, Africa, Asia, and Australia was depicted. This was accompanied by showing the solar system orbiting around the edge of the Milky way. It showed the Earth being hit by a giant object and the death of the dinosaurs and then the famous shadow figure of the rise of man.

This was followed by a picture of Earth from space in daytime and nighttime. It then zoomed in on several of the large cities. It showed several scenes of the wild.

Then it presented the range of people and the dress of the people of Earth. It gave the population of the Earth.

She presented the a few of Earths famous art, the music, and songs.

It was at this point that Janet decided to put the technical details about measure, size, hearing and seeing frequencies, numbering and alphabet that compared the Martian to the Earth equivalent. She depicted the Human standing next to a Martian.

She followed with sighting of the blackhole. The building of the Savitar. The trip out and the capture of the blackhole.

She closed with a picture of the Savitar and the ancient Martian anchor on Titan.

The Earth message part of the message was presented with the music of various cultures in the background.

Janet had engaged famous movie directors, hired the best voices, and had the technical information validated.

President Lansing's term ended but the Martian discovery kept his party in control.

He, his wife and one of their three children had chosen to move up to the Savitar. They had selected the same pentagon where Zack and Craig lived.

Emily and the President's wife Merriam were personal friends and Emily hosted a welcome aboard banquet on their arrival.

The President had a huge following on the Savitar. His support of the effort to capture the blackhole was well known.

Zack's pentagon was crowded with people when the President arrived.

Dan selected an uncovered pentagon to be the location of his Presidential Library. The covering of the pentagon would be paid for by the budget that funded the building of the Presidential Library.

Dan decided to also sponsor the building of the Zachary Milton Savitar University. The Presidential Library would be part of the campus. The garden design that each pentagon featured would be the campus common.

The Presidential Library would be at the head of the common and the pentagon's greenhouse would be opposite of it. The buildings for each college would be around the common and the farm fields would be behind each college.

There would be no tuition, but each student would be required to spend one hour of garden time each day. The number of students would depend on the available living space the Savitar could provide on campus. The initial student body would be approximately ten thousand.

Zack thanked Dan and expressed how much he appreciated the honor and the fact that another pentagon would be covered. He made sure that Sampson and "The Boss" were put in charge of all the fabrication and construction.

Janet chose to share her announced of the completion of the message to be sent a few days after the Presidents arrival. She scheduled a showing for the people on the Savitar.

She had arranged for the showing to be accompanied by special dinner events on each of the pentagons.

The total message was more than an hour and a half long and it would have the total information of Martian history as an attachment.

The reaction of the Savitar population was humbling to Janet. Her artistic and editorial skills became the center of discussion.

She had insisted her message be sent out to the Martians before it was shared with the people on Earth. She knew that there would be many people that would object to sharing so much information and would try to stop it.

Zack supported Janet. He had come to the decision to send the Martians the instructions on how to construct the laser communications systems. He concluded that a one-way speed of light message would be futile.

He worked with Conrad to provide detailed instructions on how to construct the laser and the amount of power that would be needed.

Zack worried about the power needed but he hoped that a race that had figured out how to get to where they were had made progress in the ensuing two-hundred-twenty-five million years.

He, like Janet, wanted a reply in their lifetimes.

He and his team had spent the last year preparing instructions for the construction of the system. They had written the instructions, filmed the process and had worked with the translation team to ensure the clarity of the instructions done in the Martian language.

He asked Janet to incorporate the communication instructions at the front end of her message. He wanted the recipients to know that the light speed response system instructions were included.

He and everyone involved hoped to get a response within weeks and months not in years and decades.

The transmission was designed to occur each day for ten days and aimed in such a fashion that it would create a slanted X pattern. The purpose of such a pattern was to compensate for any error in the calculation of the distance. They hoped to paint the target with the message.

Janet got the honor of pressing the initiating signal to send the message to the location out in space where they believed the Martians had gone some two-hundred-million years ago.

Now everyone would anxiously have to wait for a response.

Chapter 11: Uproar

Zack released the message sent to the Martians to Earth. There was an immediate negative backlash from many of the military powers. They believed it gave to much information to an Alien species that they did not know

The US and Europe backed the approach that Zack had taken.

It amused Zack that requests to have ambassadors on the Savitar came mostly from the adversary countries. These same countries had not been willing to recognize the Savitar as a separate independent "country". Now suddenly they wanted to send ambassadors! He knew eventually the Savitar would reach the status of an independent nation but now in the short term he declined to accept the offered "ambassadors." He had no energy to deal with a set of people that would be sent purely as spies. He preferred to wait until after the connection to the Martians had been established and then work at integrating the politics of Earth with the needs of the Savitar.

Zack instead established a twenty-four-hour listening effort. He and the rest of the Savitar population checked every morning to see if any response from the Martians had occurred.

Enrico set up a beacon in every community. The beacon would send a rotating light to shine across the roof of each pentagon enclosure if a reply came in.

Every third day Zack had the message broadcast out again. It followed the same pattern but with a slightly different aim. He recalled his duck hunting days and recalled how easy it was to miss the target. He made sure that the region they were interested in was saturated with the message.

The Martians were either alive and getting saturated with the same message or they might not be in existence.

Janet led the group that jogged with her. The group had grown from the three members that had been Zack's bodyguards to a group that had twelve to fourteen regular members that included President Lansing and his wife.

Janet was doing more running and jogging than ever before. Waiting for a reply created a tension that she had to work off.

This jogging group were the regular joggers, and most of them also participated in her Tae Kwon Do classes.

Janet and most of the group that participated in her fitness routine also participated in Emily's cooking classes. Emily was slowly turning all of them into genuine chefs.

The group had become close friends.

They knew that both Janet and Craig had a strong emotional connection with the effort to communicate with the Martians.

They were all anxious and hoped for success. Zack reminded everyone that they were reaching across more than a two-hundred million years in time and the Human evolution was a fraction of that time. Their message might find only empty space. It might be so archaic and the Martians so advanced that the comparison might be of a cave man trying to understand the picture on a computer screen.

He made the point that the human race had only been around for a million years and if they continued to constantly fight each other they might not make the next million. He posed the question if anyone thought they might last two-hundred million years.

Then it happened. They were all jogging when the light beacon began to shine and rotate across the enclosure roof.

Janet rushed back to her office.

A message had come back to them in English!

It simply said "Message Received. Detailed reply to follow."

Janet almost fainted. She sat down. Her hands trembled. She penned a reply in Martian, "Thank you for your acknowledgement. We are ecstatic to know that you have survived. We eagerly await your full reply and update of your situation."

The Savitar leadership team reviewed and approved the response.

Zack commented that the Martians must have understood his technical message and constructed the laser to signal back, or they might have already had that capability but had hesitated to reply.

He chuckled and said that if he had received the message and the part about the Earth had been the part about the Martians, he would have likely not chosen to answer.

Janet had studied the information that was still being extracted from the cube. She felt a deep connection with Nadia. She felt that Nadia's heroic life would inspire multitudes of young Earth women when they studied what Nadia had done in her lifetime.

Nadia had inspired and envisioned her as much as any living person and she had done it across millions of years.

Janet decided that she would open her own school and would become part of the University of Savitar. She set up the school of Martian Study. It would offer courses in Martian history, the Martian language, and the Martian arts.

She envisioned enrolling the Martian living on their new planet as teachers of their current social system.

It was a calling to which she was drawn. She knew she would have a lifetime of learning ahead of her.

It was at about this time that she discovered that she was pregnant. She was ecstatic. She knew that if the child was a girl, she would be named Nadia. If it was a boy, he would be Keren.

She had learned that Keren had become a key leader and builder of the Martian spaceship the Confluence. He had been a key leader in quadrupling the size of the ship. The Confluence IV Prime had become four times its original size. It had all been expanded in space with the material it had gathered as the Confluence traveled the solar system.

This by itself told of the tenacious survival spirit of the Martians.

Zack was as excited as Janet, and he let her know that he thought that the names were unique and very appropriate.

He too had continued his learning of the Martian journey through the solar system. He too was impressed with the accomplishments of the Namens family.

He figured he would share his good news with the Martians once regular communication was established.

Chapter 12: Titan Colony of Hope

Janet knew that the upcoming exploration of the ruins on Titan would be her last chance at doing so firsthand. Then she would need to worry about her pregnancy.

She and Craig planned the exploration. He would not be making this trip because he had agreed to participate with Zack in setting up the Savitar government. He also wanted to give Janet the space to get some true recognition for the groundbreaking work she had done. There was no other person other than Zack that had aided in getting this far in the quest to contact the Martians. He was super impressed with both of them.

Janet mentally envisioned the upcoming trip down to Titan and made a list of every item required at every step of the way. She knew this was her last chance at connecting with Nadia's people.

The Rama was counterbalanced with three large tanks that would hold the liquid from the seas of Titan. An additional four space shuttles outfitted to gather the materials from the rings of Saturn had also come along. Thanks to the rotating arrangement of the shuttles a one G condition was maintained on them. Their crews experienced gravity and stayed on the shuttles. This freed the Rama to be the clean room equipped vessel and still have space for the exploration team of eight and a support team of twenty.

The trip out from the Savitar to Titan took roughly a week. Then it took a day to establish the main elevator and another day to establish the fuel lift elevator.

The shuttles disconnected immediately and began the synchronous journey to gather the dry materials from the rings of Saturn. Their time was set to coordinate with the filling of the fuel tanks.

The Titan exploration team would be working on the surface for a full week but would come up to the Rama at the end of each work period. The work periods were based on twelve hours or when a specific planned task was completed. The work period could be one hour less or one hour more.

The first order of business for Janet was the erection of a sixty-foot diameter dome over the twenty-foot diameter shaft seal. This took two twelve-hour periods. The goal was to have a work area at one atmosphere of pressure so the boring cold be done with no space suit needed.

The vertical drilling machine took six hours to set up. Each six feet of drilling was followed by placing a two-inch thick ceramic liner into the hole. The diameter of the next six feet of drilling was the inside diameter of the first liner. The diameter at the top was seven feet and at the bottom of the second liner it was six foot eight inches. The team broke through to the ancient shaft drilled by the Martians just past the edge of the third liner.

The sealing cap installed by the Martians was a full eight feet thick. Upon getting a close look Janet confirmed that it was a fail-safe design that let the weight of the seal cause it to drop down when the close latches were removed.

Janet was pleased with the progress. Then just before the closing of the workday, the team discovered that an elevator blocked the way into the vertical shaft.

The team had been working for thirteen hours. She called it a day and had the newly drilled shaft sealed.

It took another thirteen-hour day to drill passed the elevator that was in the Martian portion of the shaft.

Janet was lowered down to the opening and was able to examine the bottom of the elevator. She asked the technical member of her team to create braking blocks for the four elevator gear wheels. She also asked him to have the team design a platform to be used to lower the exploration team to the bottom of the shaft.

It took the next work cycle to plumb the shaft to determine its depth and then to set up the elevator that would lower the exploration team of six people.

Janet had dutifully followed her doctor's instruction that every four hours she should lay down for one hour. She had arranged for a folding chair and a sunbathing type of beach chair to be brought down with her.

She took all the ribbing that she received from the exploration team in good spirits. She had anticipated the ribbing and felt relaxed about it and pleased that her team was bold enough to tease her.

Janet had assigned the team members not going down into the shaft to go out in the ruins of the large dome that once covered the area around the shaft and look for any artifacts that might have been left behind and that had survived through the millions of years.

The elevator was nothing more than a circular platform with railings. It was designed with three big rubber bounce wheels that touched each side of the shaft. This kept the elevator from swinging. The ride to the bottom took close to an hour.

Janet took in the long horizontal shaft to the right and a similar one to the left. Each shaft was closed with a door of the same material as the vertical shaft. However, each had a wheel that seemed to be the way to open the door. As she walked up to the wheel, the outline of a tall door about four-foot wide took shape.

She tried to turn the wheel with no luck. She looked more closely and realized that there was a curved line that was thick at one end and thin at the other. The thin end was pointing opposite from her first try.

She tried turning the wheel the other way and was surprised that it moved.

She looked at the gauge of her suit to see how much power the suit had provided. She was surprised that it only augmented her strength by five percent.

When she tried to pull open the door, she failed to do it. She had been augmented by a full hundred percent. She looked at the biggest member of her team and asked him to try.

He got it to open but had his strength augmented by a full three hundred percent.

Even so Janet was impressed that everything was still functional after so much time. It spoke volumes to her about the skill of the Martians.

Janet decided to split her six-person team into two. Three people would search each horizontal tunnel.

This suited the remaining time and it allowed for a more detailed examination of what they might find. The two teams would be in constant communication.

One three-person support team would stay at the elevator and respond to requests as needed.

Janet led the way through the door that was just wide enough to allow the exoskeleton space suits to fit through.

The exoskeleton suit featured two powerful lights mounted above the helmet that could be turned by hand controls inside the suit.

Janet walked into the first entrance on her right. Cafeteria came from her lips. She asked her two members what they saw. They both said cafeteria.

She called the other team and ask them about what they saw on their first entrance on the right. The replied that they thought it was a restaurant or cafeteria.

Janet asked them to go across the way to the entrance on the other side and she and her team would do the same.

When the team walked in, the word hospital came to her mind. Everyone agreed that there was a hospital in each tube.

Janet got the feeling that the two tubes would be duplicates. This design ensured that each tube was fully independent from the other. This approach doubled their survival chances should anything go wrong. Janet figured that living by a gasoline sea would have made her worry and ensure the survival of as many people as possible.

She directed both teams to walk all the way back to the far end of each tunnel.

When the team got there she asked them to tell her what they saw. Everyone agreed it was a super large green house. The raised tables and the hydroponic troughs were empty but still in functional condition. Everything was built from ceramic materials.

Janet could not help herself from saying out loud, "What a culture, it is as if they had just left the place."

In the back of the greenhouse, she found what she took to be a vase made out of the same stone that the tunnel was drilled through.

She had the vase boxed and prepared to go to the surface.

The walk back took them through each abode. They found a few additional artifacts; a chipped plate, a cup with a broken handle but the broken handle was inside of the cup, a chair that was almost as high as the popular high table and chair sets on earth, and in the last home a cracked mirror but the material that made the reflecting part was different from its Earthling cousin.

The other team found similar items that had been left behind. There was a brush with fur in between the brushes. This was immediately bagged for later analysis.

Janet knew that each find was a treasure of its own. She had already decided on how she would use the found vase.

She hoped the brush would yield the Martian DNA. It represented the most valuable item that had been found.

Both teams reached the side tunnel exits in unison. She made sure the doors to the tunnels were resealed. There would be many teams coming down the elevator to perform a much more detailed inspection of the Martian colonists' lives on Titan or Hope as they called this colony and the moon.

The team had been down for more than the allotted thirteen hours, but no one said a word.

Janet sat down on her lounge chair and fell asleep for the ride up. Once on the Rama she went straight to bed.

The trip back to the Savitar provided enough time for the initial evaluation of what had been found. It was clear that the colonists had taken everything of value they possessed. The information cube had made it clear that the colony on Titan was the only successful one.

Janet wondered whether she would have been able to leave the colony behind as Nadia had threatened to do. She was certain Nadia had that kind of strength. Almost single handed she had provided the iron hand decision making required to save her people.

She hoped her baby was a girl.

Chapter 13: Martian Reply

The fuel tanks were full, and the shuttles had returned loaded. Gregor Menkowski, the Savitar Logistics officer had collaborated with Victor Marquis the facilities manager and had built additional storage tanks located at what was considered the back of the Savitar. The three tanks of fuel from Titan were processed and stored in one of six tanks. The tank that took in the contents of the three tanks used to gather fuel was only twenty percent full. It would take the Rama and the Sprite many trips to fill the four tanks. Gregor worked with the engineering team to determine how long four full tanks represented for the Savitar. It did not surprise him that it represented five years of fuel.

He wondered if Zack had known this fact when he specified the size of tanks to be built. Gregor figure Zack knew.

Janet was met by Craig, and the two ships doctors. Marion and Ned were excited to have their hair on the hairbrush and had volunteered to get the hairbrush analyzed and the hair DNA determined. It would be an unbelievable achievement if they were able to get DNA samples of the Martians.

Janet took time off to get her pregnancy checked. She had taken all the precautions that had been suggested but she felt that something might be wrong.

Janet had selected Dr. Jennifer Mitchel one of ten new Drs. to have joined the Savitar as her primary care doctor. When Jennifer took an ultrasound, she found out the reason for Janet's concern and pointed to the ultrasound picture and showed Janet the beating of two tiny hearts. She was going to have twins. It was too soon to tell the gender of the fetuses, but everything was fine.

Janet was relieved and overjoyed.

Zack asked what the names would be if they were two girls or two boys.

Janet smiled and said she would wait until they could tell the genders and the two of them would decide together.

The building of The Zachary Milton Savitar University was finally getting started. The Bucky ball base that covered the pentagon was complete and the area that would hold the US Presidential library for President Daniel Lansing had been covered.

Lars, the "Boss" was now in the middle of getting the central park and the footing of the library put in. The plans called for the library to be completed in six months. The park and greenhouse would take another six months. The twelve buildings that would house the colleges would follow and go up as quickly as possible.

Dan's wife Merriam had volunteered to lead the establishment of the Savitar university.

Merriam reached out to her network and sought contributions for the university. She anticipated a huge interest in attending the university and suggested that the main campus would be the one on the Savitar but that a satellite campus would also be built in Massachusetts. This she said would make it quite easy for her to get donations to cover the expense of establishing the university. She pointed out that she would be able to solicit monies for the Earth campus and she would put a clause that part of the contributions would be spent on the materials that would make each of the colleges functional.

Her proposal was accepted, and she reached out to her many contacts to get contributions. Each college received donations. Janet's college of Martian History seemed to be the most popular and quickly reached its startup funding goal. It would be the first of the colleges to be built and staffed.

Lars reported that he had been able to double the construction staffing and that everything was going up at twice the speed that had initially been planned.

This news warmed Janet's heart because everything was coming due at the same time. It reminded her of her receiving her PhD, getting her black belt in Tae Kwon do and getting accepted into the FBI all in the same week.

This time it was having her college building and staffing and her giving birth coming due at the same time.

Ned came to one of Janet's translation meetings and shared the exciting news that the hair on the brush had yielded the Martian DNA. They too had a helix shaped chain but where humans had a single DNA ribbon, the Martians had a two-layer DNA ribbon. He theorized that such an arrangement gave the Martians better protection from radiation.

Janet asked Ned to keep this finding under wraps. She did not want anyone trying to use the DNA map to create a Martian. She asked that the DNA be tested to radiation effects and to see if mice DNA could be made to have a two-layer arrangement that would provide additional radiation protection.

Currently the radiation damage was being controlled by nano-bots. If human two-layer DNA provided radiation protection then in the near future the nano-bots would not be needed for that purpose.

The next exciting news came from Lisa. She had been experimenting with Milan's Martian plant instruction information. Milan had given the genetic maps for many of her plants.

Lisa had gathered together people in the medical field of genetics and advanced scientists in the plant world and had challenged them to create the plants Milan had encoded.

They had successfully created six different plants. Lisa had the plants growing in the new college campus greenhouse. This, she declared, was going to be her Martian greenhouse. The flowers and plants in the park were exclusively going to be Martian plants. The farmlands would eventually be growing Martian plants.

Emily had already been contacted and asked to study the translation of the Martian food recipes.

Zack had slowly closed his Presidency. He had been honored to have been elected as the first Savitar President but had quickly learned that it did not suit him.

He backed Dan for his run for to be elected the second Savitar President. There was no opposition and Dan became the second Savitar President.

The opening of his US Presidential Library and his inauguration occurred in the same month.

Dan was in his element and serious negotiations between the various countries on Earth and the Savitar got underway.

Zack pursued his new goal and partnered with Mila and Merriam to get Savitar University established.

The due date arrived. Janet and Zack were both looking forward to the delivery of the twins. Several months prior they had learned that one of the twins was a girl and one a boy. They agreed to name them Nadia and Keren in honor of the Martians they had both come to know intimately.

Janet marveled at the fact that the two came happily into the world and had not caused the extreme pain that she had heard so much about.

Life change and became more challenging. One of the first goals for her was to get back to her "fighting shape." She got back into her normal exercise routine with a goal to reach her pre-pregnancy capability and body shape.

The birth of the twins seemed to trigger action in all the activities around her. Lisa brought her a bouquet of yellow Martian "roses" that she had put in the Martian stone vase Janet had recovered on Titan.

Janet reacted by first getting tears in her eyes and after hugging Lisa asked her to take pictures. She had pictures taken of the vase and flowers, of her holding the vase and of her sitting and holding the twins with the vase on the table.

Lisa and her gardening crew had more than a dozen different Martian plants growing in the college campus greenhouse. Most of the plants were food plants. These new food plants were first being tried out on test mice to make sure they were safe for human consumption.

Emily was using her skills as a chef to prepare various recipes that had been translated.

Janet asked Lisa to make sure to keep the information about her plant breakthrough a secret.

The long-awaited response from the Martians finally came three months after the birth of the twins.

The response created excitement. It came in almost perfect English!

The message was, "Greetings, thank you for sharing your light speed communication technology.

It took us longer to translate our own long-lost language than to build the equipment following the instructions accompanying it.

Let us begin by explaining that our current alphabet has only twenty-three characters. It is very close to your twenty-six-character alphabet, but we do not have the equivalent letters for Q, X and Z. It was easier for us to translate your English message than to translate your very accurate Martian message.

Much of the information you sent to us was lost over the course of time. Our world and our two billion members all have celebrated our heroines and heroes you brought to life from our past

Nadia was legend and now she not only has new life, but we have heard her voice, her poetry and have learned of her bravery and passion for survival. We have learned of her family, of their contributions and heard their voices.

We do not possess the memory crystal you are accessing and ask that you continue to send what you discover.

The fact that your race developed on the Blue Jewel did not surprise us. The Blue Jewel was also in our legends. The fact that your rise occurred in less than a million years and much longer into the future than Nadia had ever imagined was a great surprise.

Your candid description of your history is frightening to us. We have never experienced the tenacious interactions you describe. The art and music you shared speaks to greatness, but it reflects much of the tenacity of your history. We are pleased that for the near future we have distance as our shield.

We are not yet ready to meet a race as aggressive and combative as yours still seems to be.

Your current population astounds us. We have been steadily increasing ours, but our space and resources are limited. Yet it seems to us that we have had close to a two hundred-million-year head start and have now been quickly surpassed by the newcomers.

The unbelievable ability to capture the small black hole that devastated our home world and caused our departure reaffirms our belief that you are a formidable species. You attack your adversary, and you conquer.

Your ability to create is impressive. We have strived to improve our scientific capability, but we have been humbled by what you have shared. We are sure we have much to offer in our wide area of development and look forward to sharing it with you.

After all this time we are still much the same as when we departed. Our home is on the inside surface of a huge rotating structure similar to what you refer to as the Savitar. We need the rotation to create our "gravity." Most of our world structure is still empty. The frame for the structure was built shortly after our arrival.

In the millions of years that have passed only about twenty percent of the frame has been surfaced. The lack of our ability to get more materials to create additional surface has been the limiting factor. The star providing the energy and the heat is a small red star in its dying years.

We close by updating all the technical information you shared.

We look forward to continuing the information exchange and to learning more about you as a species and as individuals. It is clear that we have much to share.

Janet was ecstatic. She knew that her college of Martian studies would have the best instructors in the universe. They would be real Martians teaching what real Martians did.

She replied with a picture of Zack, the twins Nadia and Keren and her with the stone vase and the Martian Roses. She explained the significance of her children's names and of the vase and flowers.

She went on to share that Milan's plants had been recreated and were growing and that the flowers were Martian plants and the vase had been made by Martian hands.

She shared that she had established the college of Martian studies and that she wanted to recruit a few Martian professors to teach the Blue Jewel Students about the Martian society and all things Martian.

The Martian School on the Savitar would provide professors to share the Earth Sciences and History with them in return.

Janet sent the message and knew that the two sentient civilizations that called the solar system home were on the road to new knowledge and a rich future.

The End

About the Author

Ronald E. Mueller
remwriter95@gmail.com

Ron grew up in what is now Flint River State Park in Southeast Iowa. The 170-year-old house Ron lived in is built into a hillside. It faces a 125-foot-high cliff towering over the little Flint River. The house and the land talked to him about; the passing of time, the struggle to conquer the land, the struggles people faced and the wonder of nature.

He climbed the cliffs, crawled into the caves, dove from the swimming rock, collected clams from the bottom of the pond, gigged and skinned frogs for their legs. He trapped muskrats for fur, hunted raccoons in the dead of night, and with only a stick hunted rabbits in the dead of winter.

His young life was outdoors, and nature tested him.

He walked to a one room stone schoolhouse uphill both ways. A stern but warm-hearted teacher, Mrs. Henry was instrumental in shaping his character as she shepherded him from the fourth to the eighth grade, a Montessori before its time. It was a great way to grow up.

His experiences inter-twined with snippets of fantasy lend themselves to the adventures he leads the reader through.

<u>Characters in Book</u>

First Name	Family Name	Role
Adinath	Rajkumar	Captain of the Indian Vessel.
Adrian	Moffet	Captain of the USS Sprite
Andrew	Pennington	Zack's first bodyguard, initial assassin
Benjamin	Samualson	NASA director
Bill	Masterson	FBI director
Chiang	Lee	the senior navigator
Conrad	Zepf	Science manager
Daniel	Lansing	President of the US
Dr. Craig	Garrity	Prof of Astronomy-MIT Zack's mentor and friend
Elena	Stanislav	Captain of the Russian Vessel
Emily	Garrity	Craig's wife
Enrico	Hidalgo	2nd in command. Becomes captain of the Savitar
Fred	Mathews	FBI chief, Janet's boss
Gregor	Menkowski	Logistics officer
Indira	DeSouza	Chief of Personnel. Leader of the takeover group
Janet	Romero	Zack's bodyguard, later love interest.
Jeff	Mallory	bodyguard for Craig Garrity.
Jennifer	Mitchel	Dr, Primary care
John	Adam	Shuttle pilot. Reluctant take over partner.
Lars	Mendelssohn	welding guru and unofficial leader of the welders
Lisa	Hemming	Agriculturalist in charge of the Hydroponics
Marion	Twillinger	Ship doctor
Mary	Ringhold	bodyguard for Craig Garrity.
Melanie	Baker	Samuel Trimble's business manager
Merriam	Lansing	President's wife
Mitch	Kennedy	Replacement bodyguard
Ned	McMillan	Ship doctor
Paulo	Souza	Welding manager
Quang	Nguyen	Welder - one of Zacks Farmers
Raymond	Walker	General that gets Indira onto the Savitar
Sam	Petroski	Welder - one of Zacks Farmers
Samson		Large Black man that saves Zack
Samuel	Trimble	Nano bot inventor.
Sunny	Zhao	scientist, part of the takeover network
Susan	Sanderson	Replacement bodyguard
Victor	Marquis	Facilities Manager
Zack	Milton	Main Character
Nadia	Namens	Main Character
Lamins	Evinton	Her eventual companion and mate
Lanesko	Walton	Captain
Barria	Lemin	Navigator
Perra	Laterly	Captain

Sande	Evenil	Captain
Raulen	Namens	Nadia's father-Chief Astronomer
Milan	Namens	Agronomist in charge canyon agricultural fields.
Keren	Namens	Nadia's older brother
Triansa	Evinton	Milan's longtime friend and neighbor.
Lamins	Evinton	Neighbor, eventually Nadia's lifelong companion.
Krinsar	Evinton	Lamins father.
Pend	Navel	Martian Council Leader Captain
Avian	Olens	Chief Council Science Member Captain
Halen	Welter	Captain
Mislan		Partner to Keren
Neihen		Made captain of the Confluence
Denal		Project Leader expansion of the confluence.
Meetil		One of Nadia work team
Quizl		Something like a large Guiney pig

	Sprite	the name of the US spaceship
		Captain Moffit
	Star Seeker	the name of the Chinese spaceship
		Lin Sin Pao the captain
	Rama	the name of the Indian spaceship
		Captain Adrinath Rajkumar
	Hoshi-no-ma-de	the name of the Japanese spaceship
		Hamasura Tokura
	Stremitel'noye	the name of the Russian spaceship
		Commander Elena Stanislav
	Fortune	the name of the British spaceship
		Marcus Langley Captain

Confluence

Ron Mueller

Published by: Around the World Publishing LLC.

QR Links to
ATWP.US web site

www.ingramcontent.com/pod-product-compliance
Lightning Source LLC
Chambersburg PA
CBHW070551100726
47907CB00004B/1340